THE MONASTERY

Fourteen-year-old Jake Harrison's summer vacation turns into a nightmare when his friend suddenly disappears in a field on the site of an old monastery grounds. It's up to Jake and his friends to discover the secret of the cursed abbey and locate their missing comrade— but their quest to solve the mystery leads them into horrors they never could have imagined.

Will they be able to destroy the evil force within the monastery before it's too late? And if so, at what cost? Another great horror tale by the author of *The Altar* and *Those Who Favor Fire and Other Horror Stories*.

Borgo Press Books by JAMES ARTHUR ANDERSON

The Altar: A Novel of Horror
The Illustrated Ray Bradbury: A Structuralist Reading of
    Bradbury's The Illustrated Man
The Monastery: A Novel of Horror
Out of the Shadows: A Structuralist Approach to Understanding
    the Fiction of H. P. Lovecraft
Those Who Favor Fire and Other Horror Stories

THE MONASTERY

A NOVEL OF HORROR

JAMES ARTHUR ANDERSON

THE BORGO PRESS

MMXIII

THE MONASTERY

FIRST EDITION

Published by Wildside Press LLC

www.wildsidebooks.com

DEDICATION

To Lynn Llorye

CONTENTS

THE MONASTERY

"My imagination is a monastery, and I am its monk."

—John Keats

PROLOGUE

Jake hadn't been back to Rhode Island for almost twenty years. Once he'd graduated from seminary school, he'd fled south to Miami, and his parents had retired just to his north in Deerfield Beach. He'd purposely missed all of his high school reunions, and had found a parish in the Sunshine State. He didn't miss the cold, the snow, or the bleakness of his home state. But mostly, he didn't miss the bad memories and flashbacks that had haunted him from the time he was fourteen. Since he'd left, the flashbacks had gotten better. They hadn't gone away entirely, but now they weren't so bad, only a couple of times a year, rather than the almost daily nightmares he suffered from as a kid.

Last night, sleeping in the hotel, it had all come back to him, the whole horrible story in living color, and when he woke up alone in his room, sweating and screaming, the memory had lingered, not just a memory, though, but almost as if he had relived it. And that scar in the palm of his right hand was a constant reminder that it had been real.

Now he wondered why he had agreed to perform the service. No one would have blamed him if he'd declined. But it had been written specifically on the suicide note. That was a tough thing to ignore.

He'd lost touch with his friends long ago, and no one there would even know who he was. Maybe Zack would be there, though. And Melissa. She might be there. Maybe that's why he was going. If his friends were there, he owed it to them to be there, too. From what he'd heard, they hadn't fared any better than he had. Probably worse, in fact. They'd made the mistake of staying in Rhode Island. They still had to look at that horrible monastery tower looking over Narragansett Bay. He'd seen it yesterday from the airplane as they were making their final approach for landing, and it had chilled him all over again, just like it had when he was fourteen. He'd looked up and out the window without even thinking, and, sure enough, there it had been, sticking up from the grass like a giant middle finger still trying to screw with him, even now. It had all come rushing back then, and that's probably what triggered the nightmare.

The funeral was being held at St. Kevin's, on the other side of the city, so he wouldn't have to look at it again. Thank God.

He wondered if Melissa actually would be there. She was the only good thing he could remember from that time, and although it had been just a childhood crush, it was probably still the closest thing to true love that he'd ever found. If it hadn't been for that damned monastery and the horror it had brought into their lives, things might have worked out differently. Maybe it would have been a true childhood romance that would last, one of those fairy tale things they write about in books. But probably not, he thought. It would most likely have run its course and died an uneventful death, and they would have both moved on to find adult romances. But you never knew. It was a mystery how these things worked. Maybe there really was just a single person destined to be with each of us, and maybe he had found her when he was fourteen. If it hadn't been for the monastery, who knew. God did work in mysterious ways. And apparently, he did have a plan for each of us.

If Melissa were there, he wondered what she'd be like. A middle-aged, grey-haired woman, no doubt. He'd heard that she had gone into rehab, come out clean, and married a banker. Good for her, he thought. He had even been invited to the wedding but politely declined. He had sent along a gift anyway. He still had her handwritten thank you note stashed away some-where. Every once and a while, he took it out and read it. She'd signed it, "with love, Melissa." He sometimes wondered what that meant.

And Zack. Zack's Mom had overdosed on pills a couple of years after the incident. Moving to the next town, apparently, hadn't done her any good. They'd all moved to a different town, but it wasn't far enough away. Miami was, maybe. But still the flashbacks weren't completely gone, and Jake had never been able to make anyone understand that it had been real.

Zack had been sent off to live with his grandmother, though, and he'd pretty much given up on life. He'd never finished school, which was a crime, since Zack was one of the smartest people Jake had ever known. Zack had done some time for a DWI and had also been forced into rehab. But Jake knew it hadn't worked. The last time Zack had called him, about a couple of years ago, he recalled, his friend had been drunk and incomprehensible.

And Andy…well, he didn't want to think about that.

The service was scheduled for late that afternoon. He'd ordered room service and eaten a quick breakfast. Now he had a couple of hours until he had to get ready. He sat down in an armchair by the window and looked outside. It was July 4th weekend. An anniversary, of sorts. And as he looked down at the palm of his hand, at the scar that would never let him forget, the memory of that other July 4th came flashing back again.

CHAPTER ONE

Fourteen-year-old Jake Harrison couldn't have been more than ten feet away when Andy disappeared, and if he didn't know it was impossible he would have sworn his friend had vanished into thin air.

One minute he was standing there chopping at yellow grass with the old machete they'd found in Zack's garage and jawing about how this would be the best baseball field in Warwick, even better than the new Little League field behind the Super Stop & Shop. And the next minute he was gone.

He'd turned away for just a second to sneak a look at Zack's cousin, Melissa, who he realized with both terror and satisfaction, just happened to be sneaking a look at him. It couldn't have been for more than a second or two, because as soon as Jake's dark brown eyes locked with Melissa's crystal blue ones, he immediately snapped his gaze away and his face flushed red.

That was when he realized that Andy had stopped talking, which was almost a miracle in itself. So he looked at him to see what was wrong. Only he was gone.

Jake frowned and walked slowly forward. Andy was probably playing a trick on him and was hiding in the grass, waiting to leap out and scare the crap out of him to embarrass him in front of Melissa. Both boys had their eyes on Zack's cousin all summer, but neither of them had the nerve to actually do anything about it. They were too cool to admit to wanting a girlfriend, and too shy around girls to know what to do even if they did have one. It was 1984, and despite Orwell's predictions,

Big Brother hadn't come yet, and the vast majority of fourteen-year-olds wouldn't lose their virginity for another three or four years, at least.

"Ok, Andy," he said. "The joke's over. Get outta the grass before you get covered with ticks."

He figured even the mention of ticks would send Andy screaming out of the grass; he'd found one of the ugly things embedded in his head a week before and his Mom had to drown it in alcohol and then pull it out with tweezers. Luckily, Andy's Mom was a nurse and knew what to do, but according to Andy it had still hurt like holy hell and he hadn't been too anxious to go into the field since. Jake and Zack had bullied him out there by teasing him about his phobia, but he still wouldn't have returned if Melissa hadn't been there.

Every time he did go into the field he made sure he checked himself over inch by inch before he went home, and wouldn't go to bed at night without a scalding shower that turned his fair, freckled skin even redder. So when he didn't respond to the tick scare, that's when Jake began to think that something really was wrong.

Still thinking it might be a trick, he walked cautiously to where he'd seen him last, trying to look unconcerned so Andy wouldn't think he was about to fall for the oldest trick in the book. The last thing he wanted was to look like a complete jerk with Melissa watching the whole thing.

But when Jake stepped inside the circle of hacked grass where Andy had stood just a moment before, all he found was the machete laying there on the ground as if it had just fallen from his hands.

Jake stood there for a moment while his heart did a quiet version of hopscotch. Maybe Andy had snuck off in the tall grass. But there was no trail, and a big, chunky fourteen-year-old like Andy would have left a trail, no matter how hard he tried not to.

Besides, there was the tick thing.

"Hey guys," Jake called nervously. "Has anybody seen

Andy? I can't find him."

"He was right next to you," Zack said, annoyed that the work was slowing down.

They had hoped to have the baseball field finished by the end of June so they could play ball for the rest of the summer. But it was already the July 4th weekend and the tall grass wasn't even cleared yet. If they continued at this rate, they'd be back at school before the field was finished and Zack was already beginning to get aggravated.

Jake's heart skipped again when he noticed Melissa coming over. As she stepped close enough for him to smell the fragrance of her curly, blond hair, he suddenly forgot all about Andy.

"Where'd he go, Jake?" she asked.

"I don't know. He was just here."

She frowned and brushed back a long curl from her face as she looked at him and pouted her lips in a way that made his knees shake.

Although both he and Andy had been looking at her a lot this summer, neither boy really knew how to take the next step, and Melissa actually enjoyed having the attention of two boys focused on her. As Zack strolled over to remind them of the deadline, it also reminded Jake of his deadline. If he planned on asking Melissa to be his girlfriend, he'd have to do it soon, before her parents came back from Europe in mid-August and took her away to the city and back to school, then who knew when he'd see her again. Besides, he was afraid that if he didn't make a move soon, then Andy would and might beat him to the prize. He wasn't sure what he'd do when the summer ended if he actually did get her to go out with him, but he'd at least have her phone number and Providence wasn't that far away. But he'd worry about that in September. He had to get to first base first, he thought.

"He's got to be around here somewhere," Zack said, beating at the tall grass with his rake. "Come on out, Andy! This isn't funny anymore! Quit fooling around and get out here so we can get this job finished!"

But Andy never did come out and his friends soon realized he was really missing. Melissa ran back to the house to get Zack's mom, who searched until she grew frantic and hurried back to the house to call the police.

When the police arrived, they fanned out like soldiers and searched the entire area around Zack's house, which was located right in the middle of an abandoned monastery grounds that ran for a couple of miles back, and at least a mile to each side. Zack's house itself had been part of the rectory, though it looked more like an old haunted house from the Saturday afternoon "creature feature" than a place where priests once lived. But Zack's mom liked old, spooky houses, and this one was perfect, if you were into that sort of thing.

The huge castle-like tower of the monastery loomed in the distance like a short, thick version of the Washington Monument gone black. Thick stone walls crisscrossed the area like a maze, and the grounds included an abandoned stable with the roof fallen in, a cemetery buried beneath old vines and picker bushes, and the remains of an old reform school that the monks had run years before. If you walked far enough into the woods you'd run into the west shore of Narragansett Bay, from where you could look out over the cliff and see the Conimicut Point light house.

It was a great place for boys to play and have adventures, and Andy and Jake had spent most of their last three summers at Zack's house, and now that Melissa had come to stay, they'd been there every day.

While most of the police were busy searching for Andy, some of them began asking questions and collecting evidence. The machete was placed in a sealed bag, and yellow crime scene tape was strung around the area where he was last seen. The police separated Jake, Melissa, and Zack and questioned them individually.

One cop took Jake into the back of his squad car and asked him the same questions over and over again, until the boy began to think he'd done something wrong. Did he see anyone strange in the woods lately? What were you doing when you saw him last? What were you kids doing out here with rakes and a machete? Does your mother know where you are? What was Andy wearing? Has he been acting strange lately? Had he had a fight with his parents? By the time he was done answering questions, Jake was so confused that he didn't know what he'd seen.

Andy's parents showed up just as they let Jake out of the car. They'd both had to rush home from work, and Andy's mom was so bleary-eyed and frantic that a couple of detectives had to hold her back so she wouldn't go running off into the woods looking for Andy and get lost herself. Andy's dad looked whiter than chalk as he stood quietly to one side.

Jake walked over and stood with Zack and Melissa, but they didn't say much. The police had questioned them all to the point where they were all feeling guilty, even though they didn't have anything to feel guilty about. Jake and Zack knew the area better than anybody—after all, they'd been playing there for years—but the cops wouldn't let them help, so there really wasn't much they could do but wait. Even the police dog hadn't been able to pick up a trail on their friend, but Jake was still convinced that Andy was out there in those woods somewhere.

Finally, around supper time, Jake's mom came to pick him up. When she saw all of the police cars she ran over and threw her arms around him, while he squirmed in embarrassment. Then she talked with Zack's mom for a long time before she brought Jake home.

CHAPTER TWO

Andy's disappearance made the eleven o'clock news that night, and was the talk of the Fourth of July clambake at Jake's aunt's house the next day, where the entire family gathered every year to eat steamers, crabs, roasted sweet corn and potatoes, and to tell boring stories and complain about taxes and corrupt Rhode Island politics. His parents wouldn't let him out of their sight for the entire day, which made him nearly crazy since the only other kids around were first and second graders who wanted to play baby games. He tried to teach his little cousin Stevie how to catch a baseball, but it was a lost cause, so he finally gave up and tried to hang out with the adults and act interested. And once he sat with them, they clammed up about Andy's disappearance and the men began talking about reciprocating saws and the woman discussed recipes. It was so boring Jake thought he would puke.

The day seemed endless with his parents hovering over him as if he were a newborn puppy, and he couldn't wait to get home and call up Zack to find out what was going on out there in his backyard. He tried not to think about what had happened to Andy; every time he remembered him standing there with that machete, his stomach took a dive, as if he'd just ridden the Corkscrew at Rocky Point Park. But he couldn't drive the image from his mind, no matter how hard he tried.

The police were calling it a kidnapping, and the F.B.I. had taken over the investigation. They were convinced that Andy had been taken by a pervert or something. It seemed to make sense when you heard them tell it on the news, or when you read about it in the paper, Jake thought. But if you'd been there in that field in the middle of nowhere, you'd know how impossible that story was, unless the pervert was either invisible or came from another dimension or something.

But Jake kept that opinion to himself. A kidnapping was the only explanation that made even an ounce of sense, so that must have been what happened. Even though no one could explain the absence of a struggle, or even a trail leading away from the spot, it had to be what happened.

By the time he got home from the clambake it was six o'clock and Jake watched the local news for the latest developments, while his mother called up everyone she could think of and relayed the story again to anyone who hadn't heard. About an hour later, he was finally able to call Zack, with the firm warning from his Dad not to tie up the phone.

"How'se it going?" Jake asked his friend.

"Ok," he replied, and Jake imagined him shrugging on the other end of the line. "Still no news. The place was crawling with cops until a couple of hours ago, but now they left. I think they're finished here. At least for today. They had more dogs and even a helicopter. Now they're thinking he fell into the Bay."

"What do you think happened?"

"Dunno. But I know he didn't fall in the ocean. What'd you think of that kidnapping idea?"

Jake paused. He'd known Zack since fifth grade and he'd never once made fun of anything he'd said, no matter how crazy it seemed. But he still chose his words carefully.

"I think it's bull. I was standing just a few feet away. There's no way anyone could have taken him off without one of us seeing something or hearing something."

"Yeah," Zack said. "My feelings exactly. Unless Andy ran off into the woods to hide on us...."

"Maybe. But he'd have left a trail of trampled grass. And Andy's a big kid. I don't think a perv could have got him without a fight. He would have at least screamed."

"What do you think happened?"

"I don't know. But something weird is going on out there. It's like he got beamed up on *Star Trek* or something."

"Yeah. Aliens maybe." Jake didn't laugh. Zack was serious. "Maybe we could go back out there tomorrow and check it out. Maybe we'd find something the cops missed."

"You really think my mom's gonna let me go back out in that field anytime soon? She thinks there's a perv living out there. She won't let me out of her sight."

"Yeah," Zack admitted. "My Mom's been weird, too. She thinks it's all her fault."

"Hey, it wasn't *anybody's* fault. It just happened. And who knows, maybe tomorrow Andy'll just come walking back out of the field like nothing happened."

They both laughed, but it was a nervous laugh. They both knew better.

"Well, ask your Mom if you can come over. Tell her we'll stay in the house. My Mom's home all day."

"Ok."

"Hey, Melissa wants to talk to you. Hang on."

It was a good thing Zack put the phone down because Jake suddenly lost his voice. He'd never talked to Melissa on the phone before, only to Zack, and he wasn't sure exactly what to do. Girls were a great mystery to him, and they made him intensely nervous. He never knew what to say or do around them.

A moment later, she picked up the phone as Jake managed to get his nerves together.

"Hi, Jake. You coming over tomorrow?"

"I'll try. My mom's been weird since this happened."

"Yeah. I know what you mean. But we've got to find out what happened to Andy. He might still be out there somewhere."

Jake felt a pang of jealousy, wondered if Andy had manufactured his disappearance to win favor with Melissa, and then felt guilty about thinking anything.

"I don't know. If all those cops and people couldn't find him, what makes you think we can?"

"I don't know. But there's something strange about the place. The woods, the monastery, everything. And you and Zack know the place by heart."

"Well, sort of. The woods at least. We've never been in the buildings. They've been locked up tight for years. Maybe a hundred years."

"Yeah. I found a couple of books about the history of the place that you should look at. Zack doesn't know what to make of it, but you might be able to help figure it out."

Jake heard his Dad call from the other room, reminding him not to tie up the phone.

"Where'd you find books on the place?"

"Up in the attic. The books scare me. I wanted you to take a look at them." Then she lowered her voice, probably so Zack wouldn't hear her. "Besides, I wanted to see you anyway."

Jake's voice left him again and his Dad was yelling at him again to get off the phone.

His mouth was so dry he could hardly breathe. "Maybe you can bring the books over here?"

The words came out like a croak and he was sure she was going to laugh at him, but she didn't.

"That'd be great," she said. "Zack's got to help his Mom with something tomorrow morning, so I'll sneak over around nine." She giggled. "That'll give us a chance to be alone."

"Great," he said. "Nine o'clock. Hey, I gotta go. My Dad's yelling for the phone."

"Ok, bye," she said.

Jake sat there with a dead phone to his ear, not able to believe his good luck.

CHAPTER THREE

Jake was exhausted when he crawled into bed at nine o'clock that night, and he fell asleep immediately. Two hours later, though, he woke up and couldn't get back to sleep. He went to the bathroom, then got a drink of water, but that only made matters worse. His mom and dad were already in bed with the door closed, so he went back to his room and tried not to think about what had happened to Andy, or what might happen tomorrow with Melissa. For the first time in his life, he might actually have a girlfriend. She'd encouraged him—and God knows, he needed it—so maybe if he played it right, she'd agree to go out with him. Maybe he'd get to hug her…kiss her even. He was still trying to wrap his mind around it.

For a minute he almost wished it were September so he could pull out one of those boring English books he had to read for school. That might put him to sleep, or at least take his mind off things. He had a shelf full of good books, stuff by Ray Bradbury and Edgar Rice Burroughs. But he needed something old like *The Deerslayer* or *Oliver Twist*.

Then he remembered that Melissa wouldn't be around in September, and he didn't want to think about that. Besides, if he really wanted to read something boring, all he had to do was go downstairs to his father's office and pull something off the shelf. Dad had been an English teacher for a long time until he got a new job writing things for businesses.

So he turned off the light and stared up at a white spot on the ceiling where the street lights shined through a gap in the miniblinds.

He couldn't stop himself from thinking about being alone with Melissa and it both excited and terrified him at the same time. He felt like he'd swallowed something alive and quivering, like a bag full of worms, and it rested there in the top part of his stomach just below the point where all his ribs joined together in the middle. That spot seemed to flutter and dance like a living thing whenever he thought of Melissa, and he suddenly realized it had been like that since he'd first set eyes on her. Only now it was stronger and impossible to ignore.

His thoughts wandered as he daydreamed about the next morning, and before long he found himself wondering about the books Melissa had found in the attic. He wondered what it was about them that had made her so scared. She wasn't the type to scare easily; snakes and mice and that sort of thing didn't bother her the least. He remembered the day she'd caught a black racer by the tail in Zack's backyard and it had bit her on the finger and she'd only laughed and let it go. When he thought about it, he suspected she could take most of the boys in his class in a fair fight if it ever came down to that. Not that she ever would, he thought. She might be strong, but she was all girl, soft and curvy where girls are supposed to be—he'd seen her in a swimsuit at the pool, and it was a sight that he had not forgotten.

The monastery itself had given him the creeps for years, even before Zack had moved into the rectory, but he didn't know anything about its history, other than the fact that it had once been the home to a bunch of monks. That, of course, was creepy enough, but there must be more to the story if it had spooked Melissa.

He closed his eyes and tried to ignore the strange feelings that gnawed at his insides like a dog working a bone. The last thing he remembered was that he should really get up and fix that miniblind to stop the light from the streetlamp from shining in, but maybe he'd just leave the thing alone for tonight and fool with it in the morning.

CHAPTER FOUR

The next thing Jake knew he was standing in line at the Super Stop & Shop wearing a long, brown monk's robe with a hood up over his head and the strings tied around his neck. He looked around and noticed that everyone else was wearing the same outfit, right out of the Middle Ages. The only thing different were the shoes. Some wore monks' sandals. But more wore modern shoes, sneakers, loafers, dress shoes. One woman even wore a pair of red spiked heels. Jake looked down and noticed that he was wearing his beat-up Nike's.

It didn't take long for him to realize that this wasn't the normal grocery checkout line, but the longest line he'd ever seen in his life, even worse than the line he and his Dad had stood in at Toys Я Us when he was just a kid and had gone there to see Donatello, his favorite Teenage Mutant Ninja Turtle. He remembered that line real well, waiting for hours in breathless excitement as it snaked around the toy store like some giant anaconda, winding its way past the G.I. Joes, the Tonka Trucks, and, the most agonizing part for a six-year-old boy, the Barbie dolls.

That line had been bad. But this one made it look like a television ad for fast service.

He found himself standing in the frozen food section and could sense the line twisting up and down each aisle all the way to the deli counter at the opposite end of the store. Instead of toys to look at, this line ran past nothing but row after row of food as he imagined the line going through the various aisles: after frozen food there would be bread, and then pet food, paper products, canned soups....

He had no idea what he was waiting for, but it must be good if all these people had turned out to wait in line wearing monk's pajamas. The strangest part, though, was the eerie silence. Despite the fact that thousands of people had packed the store, there wasn't a sound. It was quieter than a funeral. Or a monastery....

He guessed that they all must be waiting in line to receive communion or something, way up there at the deli counter. Maybe the Pope was there, he thought, and he almost laughed out loud as he imagined the Pope giving out blessings next to the rolls of bologna and spiced ham.

He wanted to leave, but it seemed very important that he stay in line and see what was happening, and not just stay in line, but get up there to the front quickly, before it was all over. Whatever was happening wouldn't last forever, and at this rate the store would close before he made it to the front. Besides, he couldn't bear the thought of standing in the diaper aisle, or the fresh fish aisle either, for that matter.

So he decided to sneak out of line and make his way to the end, systematically cutting in front of others whenever he had a chance.

It wasn't as hard as he thought it would be. After all, everyone looked alike, unless you stared at their shoes, and the crowd was so quiet and tame that they might have all been trained zombies.

All except Jake, or course. Jake knew exactly what he was doing.

It took fifteen minutes to worm his way into the produce department, and the deli counter was just around the next corner. The line seemed to move a little faster towards the front, as lines usually do, but he knew it was still going to be a while.

He grabbed a crisp, red apple from one of the bins, and since no one looked like they were about to stop him, he bit into the fruit. The thing tasted salty and, with disgust, Jake noticed that the inside was as red as the skin. He spit out the bloody piece he had bitten and tossed the thing onto the shelf with the celery.

As the line turned the corner, he thought he caught a glimpse of the deli counter up ahead. They had a small booth set up and, as he inched closer he saw that it was a confessional with a black velvet curtain guarding the entrance. A Stop & Shop clerk let the monks in, one at a time, but none of them ever came out again. He guessed there must be a back door or something that probably led outside to the parking lot.

He wondered why in God's name he was waiting in a mile long line just to go to confession—he could do that any Saturday afternoon at St. Kevin's and he knew what to expect with Father Barrett. A few "Hail Mary's" and "Our Fathers" and he'd be home free. He guessed his sins weren't that serious to warrant anything else.

But he still felt like he had to see this through, especially after all the trouble he'd gone through to get this far. It would only be a few more minutes. Besides, maybe it was the Pope in there. He'd waited long enough now and was too close to turn around and go back home.

The next five minutes seemed to last forever, but he was finally the next one in line. A tall monk with black, wing-tipped shoes like his dad wore went in before him, and for a moment he wondered if maybe it wasn't his dad. He strained to hear what was going on inside while he waited for the Stop & Shop clerk to tell him it was his turn, but even though there was only a velvet curtain between him and the inside, he couldn't hear a thing. Then, responding to some hidden cue that Jake couldn't pick up on, the clerk opened the curtain and motioned him inside.

The only light came from a small spotlight that shined down on a table at the left of the booth. The contrast between the harsh light and total darkness made him blink, so it took him a few seconds for his eyes to adjust and look at the table. It was a white, hard-topped thing like the cutting board his Mom used to chop vegetables, and at first he didn't realize that the thick, red gooey stuff covering it was blood.

Even as he looked up in surprise, he felt a strong, sticky hand grab his wrist and pull it down, bunching his fingers into a fist and extending only Jake's index finger. He saw the man's face looming before him as he heard something slide across the table and clamp across his hand, holding it down tightly.

The guy's face focused into the image of the butcher from the Stop & Shop. His crisp, white uniform was smeared with blood, and a stained bushel basket full of index fingers was on the floor next to his bloody shoes.

Then, before he had time to scream, he heard the whoosh of the cleaver as it descended towards his hand....

CHAPTER FIVE

Jake awoke, sweating, with a scream still on his lips and the sun shining in on his face through the gap in the blinds. He heard the clattering of dishes from the kitchen and his father's electric razor buzzing from the bathroom. His heart was pounding like a steel drum band as he slowly sat up and took his hands from under the covers to make sure all his fingers were still there.

It was with intense relief that he counted all ten.

He waited for his father to finish shaving and then got up. The fresh smell of coffee filled the house, and he heard the sounds of his mother hurrying to get the dishwasher going before she had to leave for work. His Dad was fumbling with his tie in the hallway and nodded to Jake as he went into the bathroom.

He was still shaking as he splashed his face with cold water, hoping to make the nightmare fade away, as dreams usually do. But he knew this one would linger for a long time, and might even return to haunt his sleep again.

He came out of the bathroom and walked into the kitchen just as his dad kissed his mother goodbye, then slapped his son on the back and grabbed his keys from his pocket.

"Have a good day, Jake. And stay away from that damned field."

Then he hurried out the front door.

"We've got some new cereal for breakfast," his mother said, and pointed to the cabinet. "I think I got the kind you like."

"Thanks, Mom," he said.

He watched her grab her keys and get ready to go. Then she stopped and looked at him.

"Jake, are you ok?"

"Yeah, sure, Mom. Just had a bad dream. That's all."

She raised her eyebrows.

"I dreamed I got my finger cut off. But I'm ok. Really."

Without even realizing what he was doing, he held his hands up in front of him and spread his fingers wide.

She looked at him until he put his hands down.

"Really, Mom. I'm fine."

"Ok," she said. "You call me at work if anything turns up."

He nodded.

"And Jake, you're not going back into that field, are you?"

"No, Mom. Zack and Melissa are coming over here today. We're gonna stay inside. No, I'm not going anywhere near that field."

She looked at him for what seemed like a long time, just to make sure, but he didn't drop his eyes and he didn't think mentioning that he'd be alone with Melissa was a lie. After all, Zack would be over after he'd finished his chores, and he didn't have any intention of going back into that field today. Once his mother was convinced he was sincere, she sighed.

"Ok. I'd rather you stayed around the house for a while until things settle down. If you go out, stay in the back yard and keep the gate locked."

"Ok, Mom. But don't worry. The police are still hanging around. Nothing's gonna happen."

"That poor boy's mother," she said softly. Then she hugged him quickly and left for work.

She looked back once as she walked down the driveway, and he knew it wouldn't take much for her to stay home today. And if Melissa hadn't been coming over this morning, he probably would have asked her to.

CHAPTER SIX

After his Mom left, he showered, dressed, wolfed down some of those flavored air puffs they called cereal, and waited for Melissa. To say he was nervous was the understatement of the century. He'd had crushes on girls before, going all the way back to first grade. But this was different. He really liked Melissa and wanted her to like him, too. He even made sure to put on deodorant and his best pair of jeans, even though they were tight and uncomfortable.

Finally, nine o'clock arrived, and when she didn't show up exactly on time he became even more nervous and started to pace back and forth. Zack's house was directly across the street, and every now and then he'd sneak a peak out the front window, but he didn't want her to see him looking for her so he tried to stay out of sight just in case she was coming across the road. He began to think she'd changed her mind, or that maybe Zack's Mom wouldn't let her go out.

But the doorbell rang at five after nine, and only then, as relief rushed through him, did he remember that his Mom kept all the clocks set fast so they'd never be late.

Jake let her in and motioned her to the couch in the living room and handed her a Pepsi. She put her backpack on the floor in front of her and sat down, and he watched the way the sunlight from the picture window highlighted the blond curls of her hair. She wore white shorts and a yellow pullover shirt, and a pair of pearl earrings. Jake thought she looked delicious. He felt awkward being alone in the house with a girl, and was sure that his mom would not have approved if she knew. Vaguely, he wondered what Melissa had told Zack's mother, then he decided it probably wasn't a good idea to ask.

He sat down beside her and shifted uncomfortably in his seat.

"I…I like your hair," he said, then he flushed and looked at the floor.

"Thanks," she said. "I'm glad you like it."

When he looked back up she was smiling, a smile that took his breath away.

"Do you want to go out with me?"

There. He'd said it. Blurted it out without even thinking. He looked at the floor again and waited for her to laugh at him.

"Go out…like be your girlfriend?"

She wasn't laughing.

"Yeah," he said. He was committed now. For better or worse.

She giggled and lowered her eyes.

"Sure," she said. "I've never had a boyfriend before. But I'd like you to be my boyfriend."

Then she grabbed his hand and squeezed it, sending a flash of excitement through his body, excitement like he'd never felt until now, not even after making a great catch in the outfield.

Jake nodded.

"Ok, you're my boyfriend," she said, as if it were that simple, and then she leaned over and kissed him on the cheek.

His face flushed with happiness and excitement, and he wondered what he was supposed to do next. Luckily, Melissa was a lot more relaxed than he was as she bent over and opened up her backpack.

"I need you to look at this stuff and tell me what you think," she said. "You might be my boyfriend, but Andy's my friend, too, and your friend. We have to figure out what happened to him. Besides, I'm living right next to that field for the rest of the summer, Jake, and I'm scared."

Jake's voice had disappeared when she kissed him, so he just nodded. He had no idea what the job of boyfriend consisted of, but he suspected helping to get rid of her fear was part of the role. And right then he would have done anything in the world for her. So he sat back and listened while she pulled the books from her backpack and began to explain what she'd found.

CHAPTER SEVEN

Melissa took out two books: a thick, black scrapbook, and a thin magazine-like thing.

"This one's published by the historical society," she said. "It tells about the monastery in here, and about Zack's house. It even has a picture. Zack's house was the caretaker's house for the estate."

She opened up the page to where she'd put a bookmark and pointed to the bottom of the page. It was Zack's house, all right.

"I thought the priests lived there," he said.

"They did, when it was a monastery. But the monastery and the buildings around it were originally built in the 1920s. It belonged to a millionaire by the name of Blake, and it was called Blake estates. I looked him up in the encyclopedia and it said he made his money as a smuggler and a pirate. They think he might have been involved in the slave trade, too."

"This was before it was a monastery?"

Melissa nodded.

"So this Blake guy was a pirate? Did he leave behind any buried treasure?" he asked.

"I don't know if you'd call it treasure. But I think something might be buried out there in those fields. And it might explain what happened to Andy."

Jake frowned.

"What do you mean?"

"Well, the encyclopedia didn't tell much. According to it this Blake guy made so much money that he became respectable and was elected to Congress or something. It hints that he might have been still involved in the slave trade even though it was against the law in Rhode Island. Then he disappeared and no one knows what happened to him."

"Kind of like Andy did."

"Exactly. But there's more."

She opened the large scrapbook and pushed it onto his lap.

"I think this belonged to the people who lived in the house before Zack moved in. I found it in the attic. This might be the reason they moved out."

Jake looked at the scrapbook and carefully turned the brittle pages. It contained lots of newspaper clippings and a magazine article. He knew it would take a while to read them all, so he looked up at Melissa for help.

"After Blake disappeared, the church took over the place and turned it into a monastery. That's when they opened the reform school."

Jake nodded.

"After reading these articles, I think the place is cursed. A couple of kids disappeared in the 1860s. They think they ran off to fight in the Civil War. And in the 1950s the monastery broke ties with the church and started its own religion. Like a special cult built on some middle age stuff."

"Middle age? You mean like my Dad?"

Melissa forced a laugh. "No. Like in the Middle Ages. You know. Knights and castles and stuff."

"So what happened next?"

"That's when things got really weird, according to the paper. I guess they were really into discipline and stuff. Here, look at this article. This'll explain it."

She turned the page to a yellowed copy of a story from the *Providence Journal* in 1954. It was a small piece, and judging from the page number on the top of the paper, it had been carefully hidden away in an unimportant part of the newspaper.

According to the story, the reform school had been closed down when a social worker discovered the bodies of two teenaged boys who had been tortured to death by the monks. Apparently, the place had some sort of dungeon where they disciplined kids, and it had gotten out of hand. Later on, they had found another dozen bodies buried outside the reform school next to an apple orchard. They'd closed the place down, sold off Zack's house, and the site had never been used again. And the headmaster, or head monk, or whatever he was, hanged himself in prison before they could put him on trial.

"This is creepy stuff," Jake said.

"That's not the end," she said, turning the page. "Look at this one."

There was another article, dated November 1, 1977, and it told about how a twelve-year-old boy had disappeared on the monastery grounds after he and his friend had decided to steal apples from the orchards outside the reform school. One boy had gone inside and never come out, the article said. The other kid heard him screaming and had run away. The kid insisted that after he'd bitten into one of the apples he'd stolen, it had started to bleed.

A chill ran up Jake's spine as he remembered the awful dream he'd had last night, and the bleeding apple from the produce aisle.

"You ok?" Melisa asked.

"Yeah," he said, unable to suppress a shudder. "Did they ever find the kid?"

"No. They searched the place but came up empty. The kid was a troublemaker, so they said, and they thought he had just run away from home. They never found him, and his friend wound up in a mental hospital. The reform school burned down a year or so later."

"Yeah. The ruins are still out there," Jake said. "The apple trees are gone, though."

Melissa nodded and closed the scrapbook.

"So what do you think?" he asked.

"I don't know. Like I said, this place seems cursed. But if this Blake character was a pirate and an illegal slave trader, he might have had underground tunnels between the buildings and things. That might explain Andy's disappearance. Maybe he fell into a trap door or something and wound up in a tunnel."

"Or maybe somebody pulled him in," Jake said softly.

CHAPTER EIGHT

Melissa said that Zack would be finished with his chores in about an hour, though Jake was beginning to think that he could have come along earlier and that Melissa had made some sort of arrangement with her cousin so she and Jake could be alone. At any rate, Jake was grateful for the way things had worked out. He turned on the television set and found some old Warner Brothers cartoons. Tentatively, he took her hand and held it. She looked over at him, squeezed his hand back, and leaned over to rest her head on his shoulder.

For the next hour, Jake forgot about all of his problems and experienced pure heaven. He had no idea what was on television, and couldn't have cared less. All he cared about was enjoying the soft, slightly moist feel of Melissa's fingers steepled in his, and the feather touch of her hair against his cheek. The world around them no longer mattered as they sat there on the couch with the sun shining through the picture window, bathing them in warmth and pure joy.

Even as he sat there, he knew this would be a moment he would treasure and remember for as long as he lived. Most times we don't recognize what we have until it's gone, and so we look back with regret and wish we had appreciated what we had when we had it. But sometimes we are lucky enough to recognize those moments as they happen, and so we can savor them and file them away in special places in our memory. This was one of those times for Jake. He closed his eyes and tried to capture it all and hold it tight so it wouldn't get away. For the first time, he felt confidence in himself, felt like he might actually be somebody that girls would like. But he also felt the presence of time ticking away. Instinctively, he knew that love would never be this pure, this simple ever again. Desperately, he tried to hold back time, but despite his efforts, the hour flew by much too fast.

He knew it was impossible to slow time down, and Melissa knew this too as she squeezed his hand tighter and moved closer, nuzzling against his shoulder. And even as he wished the moment could last forever—or at least a little longer—he knew it was about to end as he heard Zack's footsteps scuffling up the driveway. Jake leaned over and kissed his new girlfriend on the lips. It was a short kiss—Zack was already on the front stairs. But it was his first kiss, and the sweetest kiss he'd ever had, and ever would have.

"Hey, I hope I'm not breaking up anything," Zack said as he banged on the front door.

That's when Jake was sure that Melissa had set this up, and at that moment, he was truly in love. They stared into one another's eyes for a moment before Jake managed to reply.

"Naw, we're just watching TV and waiting for you. Come on in."

Zack immediately noticed that they were holding hands, and he grinned like he'd just learned some great secret.

"Jake's my boyfriend now," Melissa announced.

Jake blushed and asked his friend if he wanted a Pepsi.

"Sure," Zack said, taking a seat on the other side of his cousin. "So what'd you guys figure out? Are there tunnels running around underneath that old monastery or what?"

Jake shrugged and handed his friend a drink. As he sat down next to Melissa, the cartoons ended and a talk show came on. This week's topic was something about teenage runaways.

He found the remote and clicked the set off, but he knew that reality had returned to his life now, just as it had on the television.

And no remote control was going to be able to change that

channel. He looked at Melissa and wondered if life would ever be so good again.

CHAPTER NINE

The three of them talked things over and agreed that the tunnel theory was definitely worth looking into. The idea of Andy falling through some trap door and into an underground passageway was a lot more believable than thinking he had disappeared into thin air, or had been abducted by aliens or some invisible psycho. Jake remembered Mrs. Bowen teaching something about that in science class, an idea called Occam's Razor, a rule that said that the truth was usually the thing that was the most simple and made the most sense. That concept seemed to work here, he thought.

The tunnel idea was a good one. They just couldn't figure out how to act on it.

"I still think we should tell one of the detectives," Jake said. "Maybe they have some metal detectors or radar or something that could find underground tunnels. If they knew they were there, they could probably find them."

"Naw," Zack said. "Telling the cops is a waste of time. First of all, they wouldn't listen. They think we're just a bunch of dumb kids and what'da we know? And second, even if they did believe us they wouldn't do anything about it because we'd make them look bad. No, they're convinced Andy fell down the cliff and wound up in the Bay. They've got boats out there now looking for him."

"He couldn't be in the Bay," Melissa said. "We weren't anywhere near that cliff."

"Suppose Andy fell through a trap door and knocked himself

out or something," Jake insisted. "They'd have to at least listen. He might be lost in a tunnel somewhere."

"They'd pretend to listen," Zack said. "But they're not gonna be of any help."

"I agree with Zack," Melissa said, and for a moment Jake almost felt betrayed. "The cops won't listen. They didn't find any of those other kids who disappeared, did they? They always have their own ideas of what happened and they're not gonna change that."

"Besides, there's got to be more to these underground tunnels," Zack said. "I mean, how many tunnels can there be? The kids who got lost never came out. Don't you think that sooner or later they would have wandered to an exit or something?"

"Unless there's an underground maze down there," Melissa said.

"Well, if they're down there, we gotta find them," Zack insisted. "That's the only way we're gonna get Andy back. And we gotta do it ourselves."

"I just hope nothing's living down there," Melissa said. "Like maybe an animal or something."

All three of them shuddered at the thought. The idea had bothered Jake since Melissa had mentioned the tunnels, and he had imagined all sorts of things living down there, everything from vampires to sewer rats. None of the images were very appealing.

"So what do we do?" Jake asked.

"We have to find out if they exist, and find a way down there if they do."

"Do you think the library would have anything about it?" Melissa asked.

"I don't know," Zack replied. "But we're running out of time. Especially if Andy's hurt. We don't have time for the library. Besides, whoever collected this stuff in the scrapbook was pretty thorough. They probably got this stuff from the library. If there had been maps, they would have put them in the book with the rest of the stuff."

"So I guess we should start looking in the field where we last saw Andy," Jake suggested.

"No chance," Zack said. "Though that would be the easiest way. But the cops still have the area roped off with yellow tape and the detectives are hovering around like vultures. They won't let anyone near there."

"If this Blake guy really was a pirate and a smuggler, wouldn't one of the tunnels lead to the Bay?" Jake said. "That way he could unload his ships and sneak the stuff right up to his house."

"Yeah," Zack said. "If we looked along the edge of the water we might find something. We'd have to go around to the bottom of the cliff."

"How are we going to get down there, Zack?" Melissa said. "Your Mom didn't even want us coming over here. You don't know what we had to go through, Jake. We had to promise to stay inside, and we had to promise to be home for lunch…."

"Yeah, my Mom's been a pain in the neck, too. She made me promise not to leave the house, and I think she was debating whether or not to stay home from work."

The three of them looked at the floor and nodded. If they didn't find Andy soon, it was going to be a long, stressful summer.

"Jake, will your mother let you come over to our house tomorrow?" Zack said.

"I think so. As long as we stay inside. And your Mom is home so my Mom might even like the idea. But if we can't go out, what good will it do? We can't find underground tunnels from your living room."

"Maybe not," Zack said. "But we might be able to find them from the basement."

"What?"

"Hey, I know it's a long shot, but suppose one of those tunnels ended up in the basement? They might be connected to the caretaker's house. Maybe tunnels connect all the buildings on the grounds."

"It's possible," Melissa said. "It's worth a try. At least it'll give us something to do instead of just sitting around and thinking."

"Then why wait until tomorrow?" Jake said. "I'll call up my Mom at work and see if I can go over to your house this afternoon. She'll probably call your Mom, Zack, to make sure we stay inside. But we will be inside, won't we? In the basement."

"We sure will," he said as Jake reached for the phone.

CHAPTER TEN

The plan worked perfectly. Jake's mother actually sounded relieved that he'd be in a house with another adult. She called Zack's Mom, just to be sure it was ok, and Zack's mother told her that he could come over right now and she'd feed him lunch.

So they gathered the books together and went back across the street to Zack's where they stuffed themselves with tuna salad sandwiches and Coke. Jake did decline the bright, red apple that Zack's mother offered, though.

"Gives me cramps," he lied, still unable to rid himself of the memory of that awful apple from his dream.

Finally, after hanging around upstairs long enough to make it look good, Zack told his mother they were going to play downstairs in the basement.

"It's too hot up here," he complained. "And we've got some games down there we want to play."

"Ok," she said.

So they followed Zack down the wooden stairs and into the basement. The place was so old Jake was almost surprised that it had electric lights, which flashed on when Zack flipped the switch at the top of the stairs. He'd never been in Zack's basement before, and he was used to the cozy, family kind like they had in his house, which had a finished basement with paneled walls, carpeted floors, and a family room with a television, and stereo, and his Dad's office with the brand new fancy computer he worked on.

But this basement wasn't anything like that. In fact, as Zack turned on the light and Jake first looked down the stairs, all he could think of was the Edgar Allan Poe story he'd read in English class, the one where a guy walled up another guy in a wine cellar and left him there to rot.

The walls were bare fieldstone, not even finished over with concrete. The cracks between the stones had been mortared to hold them in place, but the mortar had fallen out in places and some of the bare earth had sifted through. The floor wasn't concrete, either, but was built from irregular-shaped cobblestone, a granite and fieldstone mix.

"This is creepy," Jake said.

"It's just a basement," Zack said with a shrug. "It's got a lot of old junk down here that we don't use anymore. Some of my old clothes and toys that my mom doesn't have the heart to throw away, even though I'll never use them again. You know how moms are: no matter how old you get they still think you're a baby."

"That's true," Jake said. And he couldn't help thinking about all of his old junk that his mother hung onto.

The stairs were strong enough—you could tell they'd been replaced with new wood—but the design was rickety and old fashioned. Jake felt a lot better once he'd reached the bottom and set his feet down on solid ground.

Zack's basement was larger than he'd expected, larger than the one in his house that had a playroom, family room, and his dad's office. In fact, he thought the basement was larger than the house itself, but maybe that was just an optical illusion. Unlike his basement, this one hadn't been walled off into different rooms, but was just one large rectangle. Although a couple of lights hung from the ceiling, dark shadows lurked in the corners and between the cracks where the stones were joined to make the rough-looking walls. The whole place had a sour, musty smell, as if giant mushrooms were growing in the corners.

Zack's basement was pretty empty. A small table and four chairs had been placed in the middle of the room, under a hanging light. A couch sat against one wall, and the wall on the right was cluttered with stuff piled about five feet high and covered with sheets. The outline of an old crib and a baby's highchair stuck out from one corner of the sheet. You could see that this basement was used for storage and not for living in. There was no television, or even electrical outlets for that matter.

Jake felt a chill run up his spine and he realized it was cold down here, even though it was July and probably over eighty-five degrees outside. Melissa came down the stairs behind Jake and walked over and took his hand.

"Sometimes we come down here to get cool on hot days," Melissa said. "But I don't really like it here."

"So," Jake said, trying to hide his own nervousness. "Where do we begin?"

"I guess we should spread out," Zack said. "And look for something out of the ordinary that might be the door to a secret tunnel."

"You think a flashlight would help?" Melissa said.

"Yeah. Good idea," he said and ran up the stairs, leaving Jake and Melissa alone.

"I still say it's a creepy place," Jake said.

Melissa nodded and put her arm around his waist. "You wouldn't catch me down here," she agreed.

Zack was back a minute later carrying not one, but three flashlights, and he handed one to each of them.

"Here you go. I guess we begin with the walls. If we can't find anything there, then we start looking at the floor."

Reluctantly, Jake let go of Melissa's hand and picked a wall to explore.

CHAPTER ELEVEN

Melissa took the middle, Zack took the right, and Jake took the left walls and they began examining the stones inch by inch.

"With my luck it's over there behind all the baby furniture," Zack said.

Jake began in the corner and slowly worked his way up and down the wall. The individual rocks, fieldstone and granite, were wedged into place much like the stone walls that criss-crossed the monastery grounds and the surrounding buildings, and the neighboring New England stone walls that separated property lines all over Rhode Island. He didn't really know what he was looking for, but he'd watched enough bad horror movies to think there might be some kind of hidden trigger device that would spring open a secret door like they had on all the Hollywood castles and haunted houses. So he tugged at each rock, half-expecting the wall to open up or something.

Naturally, the wall didn't open up. He hadn't really thought about the primitive technology of the 1800s, when the place was built, and about the difficulty in building such a contraption in the stone basement of the caretaker's house. They might look good in the movies, but magical doors weren't as common in real houses as they were on TV.

Still, his prying and twisting did loosen up a rock, which fell to the floor with a cloud of dust and missed his foot by inches.

"Hey, guys! I think I might have found something."

Another cloud of dust and dirt fell onto the floor as he put his hand into the hole where the rock had been. Melissa and

Zack rushed over to see what was happening, and they pulled at the surrounding stones, thinking Jake might have found an opening. But nothing else would budge, and it seemed all Jake had done was pull one of the stones loose and leave a football-sized hole in the wall.

"It's a false alarm," Zack said, surveying the damage. "Just a weak spot, I guess. We'd better try to fit it back in so my mom doesn't think we're down here digging a hole to China."

They were able to set the rock back in its place, but they had to clean up some of the spilled dirt before they finished. Still, the wall didn't look exactly the same as it had, and Jake wondered if the thing would fall out again.

Disappointed, he returned to the wall and began fingering his way along, still looking for a trigger mechanism. By now, though, all the rocks looked and felt alike, and Jake was beginning to think they were completely wasting their time. They might go over these walls a hundred times and still not know what they were looking for, even if it did exist.

"There's got to be an easier way," Jake said finally. "This is getting us nowhere."

Zack called them all over to the table in the center of the room, and they sat down in the chairs. Jake looked down at the half-finished puzzle on the table, a puzzle of a wizard and a dragon, and he mechanically fit one of the pieces into place.

"How 'bout if we draw a map?" Melissa said.

"How are we going to draw a map when we don't know where the tunnels are?" Zack asked.

"We can draw a map of the things we do know," she said. "We know where the monastery is, the ruins of the reform school, the field, the house, and the Bay. So we draw them and connect the dots. They would want to make the tunnels as straight as possible, wouldn't they?"

"So if we connect the dots, we can predict where the tunnels will be?" Zack said.

"Maybe."

"That's a great idea," Jake said, squeezing her arm. He was

beginning to realize that his new girlfriend was a lot more than just pretty.

Zack hurried up the stairs and returned a few minutes later with a pad and a pencil. He thought for a second, then began to sketch.

He began with the outline of the Bay on the top of the page, and the main road on the bottom. Then he placed the various buildings on the map, as accurately as he could: the monastery tower, the reform school ruins, the remains of the stable, the other abandoned house, the field where Andy had disappeared, and finally his own house. Then he connected all the buildings with straight lines.

"There," he said. "Connecting the monastery tower to my house leads right through the stable, and right past the spot where Andy disappeared in the field."

"That would bring it to the east wall," Jake said. "And you were right. It would end up right behind that pile of junk your mother has over there."

"I knew I should have looked there first," Zack said. "I was just trying to avoid making a big mess down here."

With a sigh, they pitched in and began moving stuff away from the wall. As soon as Jake moved a mattress away, the tunnel opening was obvious, if you knew what you were looking for. It wasn't hidden at all, but was a wooden door that looked like it led into a closet, or perhaps into a bulkhead that led outside. But they knew there was no bulkhead leading out of Zack's basement.

The three of them looked at the door for a while, an ancient oak thing that would have had plenty of stories to tell, if it could talk. Jake wondered if they would have the courage to open it. Just as Zack grabbed the iron handle, his mom called down the stairs and they all jumped in sudden panic.

"Are you kids all right down there?" she called. "You're awful quiet."

"Yeah, we're fine, Mom," Zack said. "We're just fooling with the puzzle."

"Why don't you come up here for a while? I made a fresh jug of lemonade."

"Aw, it's nice and cool down here," Zack said. "Like an air conditioner. And we're gonna play a game of Monopoly. We're ok, Mom. Really."

"I'll bring the lemonade down then."

"I'll get it for you, Aunt Joan," Melissa said quickly. And she charged up the stairs before Zack's mom could answer.

CHAPTER TWELVE

"So now that we've found it, what're we gonna do?" Jake asked, taking a glass of lemonade from Melissa.

"I guess we should open it first," Zack said. "Just to make sure it isn't just a closet."

"Well go ahead," Melissa said, gesturing towards the door. "Open it."

Zack took a long, slow swallow of his drink, then grabbed the door by the iron handle and pulled.

"It's stuck," he said, straining against the door.

Jake and Melissa tried to help but it was no use. The ancient door wouldn't budge.

"Maybe it's nailed shut," Jake said. "Is there a crowbar or something we can pry it open with?"

"Yeah," Zack said. He hurried over to the other corner of the basement where there were some old tools and pipes. He rummaged around for a minute, then came up with a rusty tire iron.

"This should do it."

Zack wedged the point of the tire iron into the crack at the edge of the door and pulled back. The wood groaned horribly, and gave a little. He moved the bar up a few inches and tried again. Once more the frame creaked. He continued the process all the way around the frame, then returned back to the middle.

"I think it'll go now. Jake, you pull the handle while I pry the edge with this."

Jake pulled and Zack pried, and the door opened with an

awful groan, popping so hard that both boys fell backward onto the floor. Jake fell against the mattress, leaving black stains all over it from where he'd gotten dust and dirt all over him earlier. They lay there on the ground, grinning, because it was obvious that this was no closet, but a secret tunnel. And somewhere inside, they knew they would find Andy.

It took a minute for the air to circulate, but it was quickly apparent that it smelled like death inside that tunnel. The three of them drew back and held their noses. Then, nervously, they shined their flashlights inside.

It was a tunnel, all right, and it looked like it went on forever. The thing resembled a mineshaft, braced up with wooden beams every few feet or so. It was just tall enough to stand up in, and about three feet wide. The walls were built of stone, just like the walls of Zack's basement. Whoever had built this tunnel had obviously gone to a lot of trouble and expense. And from the look and smell of it, no one had been inside in at least a hundred years.

"Ok," Zack said. "Who's going in?"

Jake and Melissa looked at one another.

"Why don't we call one of the detectives now?" Jake said. "Or tell your Mom. Now that we've got something to show them, they'll have to believe us."

"No," Zack said. "We've got to do this ourselves. Andy's probably just a hundred yards away. All we gotta do is go in and get him. It'll take the cops forever to do anything. Of course if you don't have the guts, I'll go in by myself."

Jake had promised his mother he wasn't going to go out and get into trouble. And he hated to break a promise. But Zack and Melissa were looking at him as if he were the world's biggest wimp. And Zack did have a point. They could go in there, find Andy, and be out before anyone knew the difference.

"I'll go with you, Zack. Melissa, you stay out here and wait."

"Hey, you're not leaving me behind just because I'm a girl. Who do you think you are, Jake Harrison?"

"Well, one of us has to stay here," Jake said. "Suppose Zack's

Mom yells down the stairs again? Besides, somebody should stay here just in case…like, we might get lost or something."

"Then you stay."

"I can't stay. This isn't even my house. It's got to be either you or Zack. You guys belong here."

"Then Zack'll stay," she insisted.

"Hey, wait a minute…"

"If you don't stay, then I'll go upstairs and tell your mom and that'll be the end of that," she said. "Besides, there's no way I'm staying down here in this creepy basement alone. I'd rather take my chances with Jake and the tunnel."

So that decided it. Jake and Melissa would go in. Each of them took a flashlight and Jake took the tire iron. But as he stepped through the doorway leading to God-knew-where, he couldn't help thinking that he was getting into something that was much bigger than he'd bargained for when he'd come over to Zack's for lunch.

CHAPTER THIRTEEN

The tunnel loomed before them, descending slightly down-ward like a mineshaft. Jake held the flashlight out in front of him with one hand, and stuffed the tire iron through his belt with the other, where it hung like a sword. Then he reached back and took Melissa's hand.

"Let's make sure we don't lose one another," he said. "I don't think either of us want to be wandering down here alone."

"Right," she said, and gave his hand a squeeze.

Jake nodded back to Zack, who didn't look too pleased with being left behind, then, with a gentle pull, he led Melissa into the tunnel.

The smell was awful, like rotting garbage and bad meat, but now that they were actually inside, Jake didn't notice it as much. His fear dulled his senses. Still, he wondered how long it would take for the smell to work its way upstairs into Zack's house and his mother began wondering if maybe the toilet had overflowed, or something had died in the basement. Mothers seemed to come equipped with an extra keen sense of smell, he thought, at least judging from his own experience.

They took a few tentative steps, and then the cobblestone floor gave way to hard-packed dirt, although the walls and ceil-ings were still made of stone and reinforced with wooden braces every ten yards or so. The tunnel looked strong, at least, and Jake wasn't worried about it caving in. That was probably the only thing he wasn't afraid of. He still worried about animals living down here—bats, rats, spiders….He wasn't wild about any of them.

"Gee, I thought Zack's basement was creepy," Jake said as they turned a small corner, which was just enough of an angle to put an end to the light coming from the open basement door behind them.

"Yeah," Melissa said. "But at least I'm not alone here. I couldn't stand being left back there all alone."

He nodded but wasn't sure if she could see him by the dim light of the flashlight.

They moved forward slowly. Jake still worried about some kind of trap or trick door like they had in Egyptian tombs to catch tomb robbers. He remembered the Indiana Jones movie and all the traps the hero had to go through to escape from a similar tunnel. For a moment he could almost imagine himself as a hero fighting against some unknown evil force, and with a beautiful girl holding onto his hand for dear life. Then he remembered that he was scared to death. All he wanted to do was find Andy and get the hell out of there.

The Indiana Jones fantasy shifted suddenly as his flashlight beam stopped on something resting on the floor directly ahead.

"What is it?" Melissa asked.

"I don't know," he said, approaching the object cautiously.

The thing looked like an animal—or at least something that had once been an animal. He shined the flashlight beam down its length until it rested on a striped tail.

"A raccoon," he said. "It's just a dead raccoon."

Yet it was soon clear that the thing hadn't died recently, but it wasn't a skeleton, either. The creature almost looked mummi-fied—no, fossilized was more like it. The shape was perfectly intact, right down to the whiskers. And its face was contorted into a horrible expression of pain and fear.

He gently touched the thing with the toe of his sneaker and the body suddenly disintegrated into a pile of white-grey ash.

"Ugh!" Melissa said, and pulled him away from the cloud of dust the thing had set off into the air. "I wonder what happened to him?"

"I don't think I want to know," he said, and the word "petri-fied" came to mind—not petrified as in fossilized, though, but petrified as in scared to death.

Although he would have liked nothing better than to have turned around and run like the devil back to Zack's basement, the idea of chickening out in front of Melissa was probably more terrifying than facing whatever lie ahead. So he waited for the dust to settle, and then they went forward once again.

After they'd walked maybe 50 yards or so, they came to a fork in the tunnel, with wooden doors barring each of the paths. One seemed to go slightly to the left, and the other slightly to the right.

"We should have brought Zack's map with us," Melissa said. "It might have given us some idea where we are."

"I bet one of them leads upstairs to the stables," Jake said. "Probably the left one."

Melissa nodded as they looked at each other.

"You're not thinking of splitting up, are you?" she said. "Because I'm not going anywhere without you."

He smiled. "I wouldn't think of it. Let's try going to the right. Here, you grab the handle while I pry at it with the tire iron. This thing doesn't look like it'll open any easier than the last one."

It took just a few minutes to wedge the door open, and then Jake led his girlfriend through the door and into this new passageway.

Neither of them heard the door slam shut behind them.

CHAPTER FOURTEEN

As soon as Jake moved into this new tunnel he had the immediate feeling that the place had suddenly become much larger. The smell wasn't as bad here, and this passageway was higher and wider, and the walls had a more polished, finished look. He could feel the air circulating through this tunnel and guessed that, somewhere, it opened up to the outside and generated air currents of its own.

"I think we might be underneath the field soon," Melissa said. "It's just on the other side of the stable."

"Yeah. Maybe we'll find some sign that Andy was here," he said, sweeping the flashlight across the floor. "We'll have to keep our eyes open."

He knelt down and touched the ground. It was packed down even harder here, almost like cement.

"We won't find any footprints here. An elephant could have run through and we'd never know it."

"Not unless he had to stop and go to the bathroom," Melissa replied.

Jake couldn't help snickering at the image as he stood up and looked ahead into the darkness. The tunnel was wide enough that they could walk next to each other now, so he took Melissa's hand and moved on, walking slowly and carefully to avoid any traps or danger, and to make sure they wouldn't miss any signs of Andy.

They'd traveled maybe another fifty yards or so when Melissa pointed her flashlight at the wall just ahead.

"What's that?" she said, pointing to where the beam glinted off something at the base of the wall.

As they moved closer, Jake saw that it was a small, gold crucifix.

"It's Andy's all right!" he said, picking it up and turning it over. "His initials are engraved on the back. Father Barrett brought this back for him from Rome at Christmas. All of the altar boys got one. Andy never went anywhere without it."

"It's missing the chain," Melissa pointed out.

"It must have come loose."

"Either that or he left it behind for somebody to find."

"Maybe," he said. "But the important thing is that Andy was here. Now we know for sure. We're on his trail. I just wish I knew how long ago he left this."

"Yeah," Melissa said, slapping his shoulder. "He was here. And we must be going the right way or else we would have run into him on the way here."

"Besides, the door we came through was wedged shut and Andy didn't have a tire iron to open it with."

Jake felt excitement burning in his chest as he realized that they'd been right all along, and that Andy actually was down here somewhere. They might just be dumb kids, but they'd outsmarted the police and the detectives. They'd been right all along.

Now all they had to do was find their friend. Jake had no idea how Andy had gotten here, and he didn't want to think about it at the moment, but they were on his trail, all right.

It was just a matter of time now, and he thought that even if they did get in trouble for coming down here, it would all be worth it.

"Let's get going and find him," Melissa said. "This tunnel can't go on too much farther. And I want to get the hell out of here."

"Gotcha," he said, and put the crucifix in his pocket. "Come on then."

They moved forward again and tried not to think about how

the tunnel seemed to dig itself deeper into the earth, and how the air grew colder and damper with each step.

CHAPTER FIFTEEN

It wasn't long before they came to another branch in the tunnel and another door and once again they had to decide which way to go.

"At least this one isn't locked up," Jake said.

"No, but if it was it would be easier to find Andy. We'd know he didn't go that way."

"Yeah. So which way do we go?"

"Eenie, meenie, minee, moe," Melissa said. "We might as well flip a coin."

"I don't have a coin. Pick."

She looked back and forth at the two passageways, then finally pointed to the left.

"This way," she said. "It feels lucky."

So they went left. It was as good a choice as any, and he wasn't about to rely on his luck to guide us.

The tunnel took a sharp turn, and Melissa gasped as their flashlights illuminated a white, grinning skull just ahead.

They both took a step backward, startled by the sudden vision of horror, and they saw that the skull was attached to an entire skeleton, bleached white by time and sitting upright against the wall and staring at them through deep, hollow sockets.

"It's ok," Jake said, as much to calm his own fears as to reassure Melissa. "It's dead. It can't hurt us."

"It's not Andy?"

"No," he said. "It's too old. This thing's been here a while."

Jake moved closer to the skeleton, but Melissa refused to

budge. It had been a kid, judging from its size. The clothes had long since rotted from its form, but a metal belt buckle rested at its waist. And some metal buttons had spilled to the ground beside it.

"It's definitely not Andy," he said.

"Thank God."

Jake moved away from the skeleton and took her hand again.

"Do you think he came this way?" she asked.

He looked around quickly, scanning the floor with his flashlight. Then his eyes stopped on another shiny object. He took a step closer and picked it up. It was the chain that Andy's crucifix had hung from.

"Yeah," he said, holding the chain up. "He was here all right. It must have broken and fallen here."

"We're still going the right way, then."

"Yeah. Come on. This thing gives me the creeps, even if it is dead."

"I've never seen anyone dead before," Melissa said softly. "Especially not a kid. Even if it is a skeleton, it was a kid once."

"Yeah. I never seen anyone dead before either. Let's go. We don't want to think about that now."

They went around another corner, then came to another split in the tunnel. They took the left passage again, and soon found themselves going down a set of stone stairs leading even deeper beneath the ground.

CHAPTER SIXTEEN

As he and Melissa went down the stairs, the excitement Jake had felt at finding Andy's crucifix turned to fear. He couldn't put his finger on it, but the idea of going down deeper into the earth terrified him nearly to death. Naturally, he didn't let on to Melissa that he was scared. But if he'd had his way he would have turned around and run all the way back to Zack's basement.

It was almost as if he knew things were going to get bad.

The stairs led to another door, a heavy wooden thing that looked even older than the ones they had already passed. Its thick hinges were red with rust, and the iron handle was almost brittle to the touch as it dared Jake to open the door. He looked at the thing and felt a coldness eat away at his spine. And he looked over at Melissa as he felt her trembling beside him, her angel-like face silhouetted in the bad light.

"What do you think?" he asked, trying to break the tension.

"I don't want to go in there."

He took a deep breath.

"Why don't you go back?" he suggested. "Go back and get some help. I'll keep going. He's probably right on the other side of this door. But if you go back you can get the cops and maybe a doctor and they'll be there if we need them. When you get back you'll probably find Andy and me down here toasting marshmallows."

She forced a smile and shook her head.

"I'm not going anywhere by myself."

Jake felt a mixture of both relief and guilt, but it was mostly relief. He didn't want to go in there any more than she did, and he sure didn't want to go in there alone. In fact, he really wanted both of them to go back and get help. But time might be a priceless commodity, and Andy could be in real trouble now. He probably hadn't had anything to eat or drink, and he might he hurt or sick. Every minute could count now, and Jake would never be able to forgive himself if his friend died because he was too afraid to keep going and find him. No. They had come this far. They couldn't go back now. Not until they knew.

"Then I guess we've got to do it together," he said, grabbing the rusty handle.

Unlike the other doors they'd come to, this one opened easily, even as the handle fell off in his fingers. Jake knew that Andy had been here before. And he somehow knew they were walking into something that no kid should have to face. He felt it in his bones, in the pit of his stomach, in the dryness at the back of his throat. But he had no way of knowing how bad it would really be.

The doorway led into another tunnel, which seemed to open into a larger room just ahead and away from their flashlight beams. A yellow, flickering light shone out from this room, and Jake and Melissa both pulled back inside the doorway and yanked their flashlights back.

"There's somebody in there," Jake whispered. "There's lights on."

"It's Andy!" she said, and lunged forward.

Jake pulled her back.

"What if it's not," he said. "What if it's a perv or something?"

"But...."

"No. Turn off the flashlight. Let's be careful. Let's sneak in, just in case."

Melissa nodded. Then they dropped to their knees and stuck their heads through the doorway. Jake's bad feeling only got worse.

CHAPTER SEVENTEEN

They crawled forward like weasels heading towards the distant light. It was a yellowish, flickering light, probably a fireplace or torch, Jake supposed. The electricity had been turned off in the buildings years before, he remembered, thinking back to Melissa's newspaper clippings.

As they crept closer, they saw another door between them and the light, right near the end of the tunnel and leading into the room. This door had been left open, either by mistake or maybe as an invitation. Or maybe it was a trap.

They stopped just inside the door and rested for a minute. Jake tried to make his heart stop beating so hard, but he might just as well tried to make the sun fall from the sky. They rested there in silence, afraid to peek too far into the room, yet knowing they couldn't just lie there forever.

He motioned for Melissa to back away from the doorway. Then he crawled forward another couple of feet until he could clearly see into the room.

The light came from firelight, as he had thought, as several lit torches flickered from the walls where they neatly sat in metal holders like flagpoles lining the room. It took him a few seconds to get his bearings, but then he realized he wasn't looking at the room from ground level, as he had first thought. Another set of stairs sloped downward ahead of him—he could have reached out and touched the first step. A dozen or so more steps led down and into the room, and Jake realized he was looking down at it from about the height of a basketball hoop. And the ceiling was still high above him.

The walls of this room had been built of stone, but not the small stones they had seen in the tunnels. These huge, brick-shaped stones resembled cinderblocks, and the way they were neatly stacked like Lego blocks made the room look like the inside of an ancient castle.

No, he thought suddenly as he realized what he was looking at. Not a castle. A dungeon.

Jake looked down at the room in disbelief and thought for a moment that he'd been transported back in time to the Spanish Inquisition. He'd seen a movie about it somewhere on television, and he remembered it from "The Pit and the Pendulum," which he read in English class. It was a dungeon, all right, complete with a collection of torture devices that would have made Freddy Krueger drool.

Chains and manacles hung from the wall, along with something that looked like a metal bird cage. Jake didn't think the thing was designed to hold an ostrich. Especially when he noticed a human skeleton clutching to the bars. He saw what looked like a row of thumbscrews, in various sizes, he supposed, and a huge axe that could have taken a man's head off with a single chop. Beside that was a knife collection the likes of which would shame the equipment of even the world's greatest chef. There were pokers and swords, and a cauldron-like kettle with hot, glowing coals and pointed things sticking into it like toothpicks. He saw a rack, and one of those pillory things they used on the witches at Salem. Beside the cauldron stood a huge, wooden table with chains and iron manacles to hold someone down. It was probably a primitive operating table, Jake thought, the kind they used before they'd invented anesthesia. As he slowly scanned the room, his eyes bugged out in amazement as he looked at some terrible things he recognized, and others whose use he could only guess.

Finally, his eyes stopped at the far right of the room, and for a moment he just lay there on his belly and stared, not knowing if what he saw was real, or just some weird hallucination. Jake gasped. He wondered if he were still dreaming, maybe a continuation of the nightmare he'd had about the Stop & Shop. He shook his head, hoping he'd wake up and it would go away.

But it didn't.

It was Andy, and he was chained to the wall with iron manacles clamped tightly to his wrists and ankles.

His skin was whiter than paste, and his head slumped over to one side. His eyes were closed, and Jake couldn't help thinking of how his friend looked like Jesus on that gold cross he now had in his pocket.

Except Andy was wearing jeans and the same Boston Red Sox shirt he'd had on when he disappeared in the field just two days ago.

"Oh my God!" he whispered, and he could feel Melissa's body pull up beside him.

"It's Andy," he said softly, and pointed to the spot. "Over there. Somebody's got him chained to the wall."

Melissa made a strange, painful sound in her throat. Then she ducked back and buried her face in her arms.

"Can you see anyone else? Or anything?"

"No. Whoever chained him up is gone, I think. At least for now."

She lifted her face up and stretched forward for another look.

"Oh my God," she breathed. "Is he still alive?"

"I don't know. I can't tell. But we can't just leave him here."

Jake thought about calling out to him to see if he'd respond. But that might attract the attention of whoever had caught him, and he didn't want to deal with that problem just yet.

"There must be some sicko living down here," he whispered. "Like in *Phantom of the Opera*. Only in a monastery."

"Maybe they're holding him for ransom or something."

"Maybe. But wouldn't they have asked his mom for money by now?"

"I guess. What're we gonna do, Jake?"

But before he could answer, a door opened on the other side of the room, one he hadn't noticed before, and a hooded figure in a brown monk's robe stepped into the room, carrying a steaming bowl of soup in his hands.

CHAPTER EIGHTEEN

Jake held his breath in fear as the monk-like figure entered the room, walking slowly so as to not spill the soup and wearing exactly the same outfit as Jake had worn in his nightmare. He shuddered as the monk placed the bowl down on the operating table and walked over to where Andy was chained.

Although he couldn't see the monk's face in the bad light, his white beard stuck out over his throat, making him look like a twisted version of Santa Claus only wearing brown instead of red. But he immediately knew that this guy wasn't a jolly old elf as he looked up at Andy, then slapped him hard across the face with the back of his hand.

Andy groaned and slowly opened his eyes. Even from across the room, Jake could see that Andy wasn't afraid, and he felt proud of his friend. His eyes looked glazed and resigned, but not afraid. And though his body looked like it had been racked with pain, and fresh blood flowed from his cheek where the monk's ring had cut him, he refused to cry out, but just looked at his tormenter through blank eyes.

"Wake up, my little friend," the monk said in a raspy voice.

"Leave me alone, you perv," Andy said, and Jake was surprised at how well his weak, trembling voice carried across the room.

The monk laughed. "I thought you might want your supper."

"I'm not hungry."

"Ah, but I'm afraid you must eat," the monk said. "I have to keep you alive until midnight. After that, it won't matter anymore. At least not to you."

"Just get it over with now, you creep," Andy replied, and Jake actually thought he wanted the monk to kill him then and there and be done with it. Then, as if to provoke his tormenter into actually doing it, he spit right into the monk's face.

The hooded man exploded in fury and viciously slapped Andy again.

"Oh, you'll regret that, little boy!" he said, and grabbed an ugly looking bullwhip from the torture collection. "I will make you hurt. Make no mistake about it."

Then he whipped Andy, first across the legs, and then across the chest until the blood flowed and stained through his clothes.

Andy tried not to scream, but the pain was too much and he let out a blood-curdling yell. Jake wondered how the police couldn't have heard it out there in that baseball field the boys had been building. Jake felt the hairs rise up on the back of his neck, and he tried to look away but couldn't as the monk threw the whip down and grabbed a small axe from his collection.

"Don't worry," the monk said, taking a set of keys from inside his robe and unchaining Andy's hands and feet. "I'm not going to kill you. I'm keeping you alive until midnight. But I can sure make you wish you were dead."

He dragged Andy over to the operating table and threw him onto it, almost spilling the soup in the process. He clamped the boy's hands and feet to the straps, then hefted the axe over Andy's right hand.

"What do you say? Maybe we'll begin with the little finger? Then we can work our way inward."

"No!" Andy screamed. "No! Please don't! I'll do anything you want. I promise. Anything."

The monk watched him for a moment and seemed to weigh the possibilities in his mind, undecided about what to do. It was almost like he was listening to voices, Jake thought. Finally, almost reluctantly, he put the axe down and picked up a spoon.

"That's better," he said. "Now you're going to eat this nice soup I cooked."

As Andy nodded, Jake felt Melissa tugging on his arm.

He looked at her and she motioned him back into the darkness of the tunnel. He took one last look at the monk, who was now gently spooning broth into Andy's mouth, as if he were a baby in a crib, and then Jake moved away, very slowly, and very, very quietly.

CHAPTER NINETEEN

They crawled all the way back through the tunnel in complete darkness until they reached the main corridor. Only after they had squirmed through the doorway and Jake had gently eased the aging door closed did they dare turn their flashlights back on.

"Jake, we gotta get back to the house and get help now!" Melissa said. "This guy's crazy! He's a nut-case. He's gonna kill Andy at midnight."

"We can't just go off and leave him there with that wacko."

"We have to. He's gonna kill him. But not until midnight. That gives us enough time to get help and then come back down here and get Andy out."

Jake nodded. He'd forgotten his watch and had no idea what time it was, but he was sure it was nowhere near midnight.

"You're right. We have time. But what if nobody listens to us?"

"We'll make them listen. You can show them Andy's crucifix. Come on. Let's get out of here before that crazy monk finds us here and locks us up in his dungeon too."

Just the thought sent a chill up his spine and he didn't need any more encouragement as Melissa grabbed his hand and led him back towards Zack's basement.

They hurried back the way they had come. As they passed the skeleton, Jake looked at it with new insight and wondered if this kid had been a guest in the monk's torture chamber, too. The place was right out of the Spanish Inquisition, and he imagined this crazy monk might have thought himself the grand inquisitor. He'd read a little about it and couldn't remember the guy's name, but he vowed to look it up again if he lived long enough to get back to his books.

For some reason, it didn't take as long returning as it did coming. They didn't need to be so careful this time—they knew where the danger was. So even before he had time to realize where they were, Jake found himself staring at the last door, the one leading through the short tunnel that opened into Zack's basement. He could imagine Zack, just fifty yards away, waiting for them, pacing back and forth in the basement and wondering what in God's name was happening in the tunnels.

Only this time, he realized with sudden horror, the door was closed.

He and Melissa looked at each other.

"The wind must have closed it," he said nervously, and pushed at the door.

It wouldn't budge. Not an inch.

He pushed harder. Still nothing. He pushed with every ounce of strength he had.

It didn't move.

"Give me a hand," he said, really worried now, and Melissa squeezed in beside him. Together, they shoved and heaved at the door.

As soon as he'd touched the thing he'd known it wasn't going to open, and no amount of force was going to make it open. But he had to try anyway, hoping against all hope that he was wrong.

"It's really jammed," Melissa said. "Try the crowbar."

He pulled the tire iron from his belt and pried it into the crack at the edge of the door. He pulled and Melissa pushed, but the door didn't move one bit. Finally, they desperately threw themselves against it, banging it again and again with their shoulders until they both collapsed on the ground, exhausted and frustrated.

"What'd we do now?" he asked, and whacked the door with

the crowbar one last time, just for good measure. Although hitting the thing relieved some of his anger, he might as well have beaten the door with a banana.

"You think Zack can hear us?" Melissa asked. "Maybe if we scream loud enough…."

He shrugged. "I doubt it. And if we scream, that crazy monk might hear us too. Maybe he's already heard us…."

As soon as he said it, he knew it was a mistake. Melissa buried her head in her hands and tried real hard not to cry. But it didn't work, and Jake was glad it was dark and she wasn't looking, because he had tears running down his own face as well.

"It's ok," he said, patting her shoulder. "He can't hear us. If he could, he'd have been here already."

"I hope you're right," she said, wiping her eyes on her sleeve. "So what do we do now?"

"We can't get into the basement," he said. "So I guess we have to go back to the dungeon. That must be underneath the monastery tower. Maybe the monk will leave and we can set Andy free while he's gone. We can watch from the tunnel. I don't think he can see us there and we should be all right as long as we can stay quiet."

"I just hope he can't hear the beating of my heart," Melissa said.

"Yeah. Mine too."

They stood there for a moment and thought.

"What about the other tunnel?" Melissa said, finally. "The one leading up to the stable."

Jake slapped his head. "That's right! We could try that one and maybe escape through the stable. Why didn't I think of that?"

"Because you're a boy," Melissa said.

"Very funny," Jake said. But he was relieved that they now had a plan 'B'. "Come on. We may be able to get out of here after all."

CHAPTER TWENTY

They turned away from the door that would have led them to safety if only they'd been able to open it, and instead they moved deeper into the tunnel once again. Neither of them spoke as they retraced their steps and came to the first branch of the tunnel. The door they'd gone through was open. The other one was closed.

"Well, here goes," Jake said, grabbing the handle.

Much to his relief, this door opened easily. He didn't even have to use the tire iron. It creaked slightly as he pulled it open and he squeezed his head through the doorway.

His flashlight showed a steep set of grey, granite steps leading upwards, like tombstones set on their sides and piled up. It reminded him of a basement bulkhead, only much older, much narrower, and much creepier.

"It goes up," he said, stating the obvious, and Melissa poked her head in to check it out for herself.

He led the way up the narrow staircase and tried not to imagine the damp, stone walls closing in on him, pressing him from all sides like some giant vice. The steps were almost as steep as a ladder and led straight up to the ceiling. Jake stopped and followed the stairs with his flashlight until he saw a break in the ceiling that looked like a hatch.

"It must be a trapdoor on the floor of the stable," Melissa said.

He nodded and motioned her to come up beside him.

"Let's get it open and get out of here," he said.

Jake moved up towards the ceiling, hunching down so his

shoulder was against the door. Bracing himself against the wall, he pushed upward, easily at first, and then with more force.

"Here we go again," he said, as nothing happened. "The door won't move an inch."

The passageway was too narrow for Melissa to be able to help him push, and the stairs were damp and slippery. She jammed herself behind him, though, and pushed against Jake as he shoved against the door. They heaved at the thing, again and again, until Jake's feet slipped and he almost went down. Melissa managed to catch him as they both painfully whacked into the wall.

By now Jake wasn't cold anymore. The sweat was pouring from him like a river, both from pushing against the door and from a lingering fear that maybe the crazy monk had heard them and was already setting his trap to capture them and carry them down into his dungeon. Angry, he shoved himself at the door one last time, and once again he would have fallen if Melissa hadn't braced him just in time.

"It's no use," he said finally. "We're gonna break our necks up here on these stairs."

"There's a ton of stuff in that old stable," she said. "The roof and one of the stone walls have fallen in. All that junk is probably on top of that door and that's why it won't open."

"Yeah," he said, and groaned as he realized that he'd banged his right elbow pretty hard on the wall. "But what do we do now?"

"I don't think we have any choice," she said. "We're gonna have to go back to that dungeon and wait for the monk to leave. Then we'll go in and try to get Andy free."

"How're we gonna get out once we do have him free?" Jake said, as if the task were that easy and had already been done.

Melissa shrugged. "Maybe Andy can show us how he got in. Or we can follow the tunnel past the monastery and see if it really does lead out to the Bay like we thought."

"I'm sure it must. I just hope we don't get lost trying to find our way out. Or that the opening at the other end isn't locked shut, too."

"Yeah. But we're getting ahead of ourselves. And remember, Andy got in somehow. Before we can worry about getting out, we've got to get Andy out of that dungeon. If we stay down here too much longer it'll be midnight and it'll be too late anyway."

"I wish I'd worn my watch." Jake was worrying about what would happen when his parents got home. Maybe then they'd come looking for them. Zack would have to tell them what happened and they'd come down looking for them.

And maybe the monk would change his mind and kill Andy before midnight if somebody came looking. Either way, they had to act. They had to do something.

So they climbed back down the stairs and went back toward the dungeon. Jake wondered about how Andy had gotten down here, and he decided there must be another trap door somewhere, maybe leading up to the field. But they couldn't take the time to search for it now. And as they turned the corner leading to the dungeon tunnel, he couldn't help wondering how old the batteries were in their flashlights.

"Turn your light off," he told Melissa, and he took her hand. "We might need it later if the batteries are low. We'll just use one light now."

She nodded and put the light into her back pocket and allowed Jake to lead the way. He just hoped he wouldn't let her down.

CHAPTER TWENTY-ONE

They closed in on the dungeon sooner than Jake would have liked, retracing their footsteps until they came to the last tunnel. Melissa took the flashlight out of her pocket and placed it next to the door leading in. He nodded in approval; once inside, they wouldn't need the extra flashlight, but it might come in handy here if they needed to make a quick getaway and he'd lost his light. He grabbed the door with one hand and opened it as he turned off his own flashlight with the other, plunging them into total darkness, except for the flickering light of the torches from the dungeon at the end of the corridor.

Just as he was about to kneel down and begin the long crawl towards the dungeon, he felt Melissa slip her arms around him and pull him close. He hugged her back, holding her for a long, wonderful minute. Squeezing her tight, he closed his eyes and cherished the moment, not knowing what awaited them next.

"No matter what happens, Jake, thanks," she whispered in his ear, so softly he could barely hear her. Then she said something else, even softer, and though he couldn't be sure, Jake thought she told him she loved him. Before he could respond, she had broken away from him, and the next thing he knew, they were both on their hands and knees, crawling on their bellies like worms towards the light.

When they reached the entrance to the dungeon, he carefully peeked his head forward and peered into the room. It was pretty much the same as when they'd left, only Jake didn't see any sign of the monk. Andy lay on his back on the operating table where he'd last seen him. Both the axe and the bowl of soup were gone, and Jake quickly looked around the room to see if the monk might be lurking around somewhere.

He looked into every shadow, every corner, and though he imagined him lurking everywhere, he couldn't find him in the dungeon. He half expected him to be hiding somewhere, waiting for them to come in, and then he'd jump out and grab them, too. Maybe he was feeling a little paranoid, but under the circumstances, he supposed it was justified.

"He's gone," he whispered to Melissa. "Take a look."

She crawled up beside him and took her time scanning the room, too. Finally, she nodded.

"He's gone," she said. "But for how long? He could be back any second. We're gonna have to hurry."

Jake noticed that the door the monk had come through was closed. He nodded. It was the perfect chance, especially since Andy was just strapped to the table and not locked to the wall in manacles that they didn't have a key to. That, at least, was a lucky break.

"Come on," he said, and scampered down the stairs, trying to keep his pounding heart in check.

Melissa followed closely and they hurried down into the dungeon itself and ducked behind some torture devices just to make sure it hadn't been a trap after all. Jake was surprised and relieved to see that the monk didn't jump out from someplace and pounce on them.

The place smelled like a combination of rubbing alcohol and rotten meat, with a bushel or two of moldy lettuce thrown in, just for good measure. Jake looked up and made sure the door the monk had come through was still closed. It was, and he breathed a sigh of relief. He and Melissa looked at each other and forced a smile before they scuttled over to the table where Andy was strapped down.

Melissa began fiddling with the straps while Jake tried to wake his friend up.

"Andy, wake up!" he said, trying to keep his voice low as

he gently shook his friend. "It's Jake. And Melissa's with me. We're gonna get you outta here. Come on, man, wake up."

Groggily, he opened his eyes and blinked in disbelief. Jake placed his finger to his lips, motioning him to silence.

"Shhh! You're not dreaming. It's really us. We're gonna get you out of here."

Melissa was working on the last strap now, the one that held down his right hand. She released the catch and Andy was free.

"I...I don't think I can walk, Jake," he whispered, wincing in pain. "I'm not even sure I can move."

"You have to move," Jake said. "You don't have a choice. I don't care how much it hurts, it's better than staying here, isn't it? He's gonna kill you, man. Don't you get it? You've got to get out of here and now's your only chance."

"Yeah, Jake. I know. He's gonna kill me tonight. I think he's gonna cut me up and feed me to some creature or something. It's some kind of weird ritual he does. He's gotta wait until the moon's right or it won't work. Believe me, I want to get outta here more than anything. I just don't know if I can make it."

"We'll help you," he said, and tried to slide him to the edge of the table so he could get down. That's when they heard it.

Even then, Jake never would have picked up on it ordinarily. But his nerves were raw with fear and he was wound up so tight he thought he could have heard mice sleeping.

The sound came from outside the door where the monk had come from before. The madman was on his way back. Jake knew it as sure as if he'd had X-ray eyes.

"He's coming!" he said. "Hide!"

He and Melissa both bolted for cover as the door creaked open.

CHAPTER TWENTY-TWO

Somehow, they made it.

Even as the door groaned open, Jake dived behind a large wheel-like contraption that you strapped somebody to and then spun it around until they threw up. He supposed you could kill them if you spun the thing long enough or hard enough, but for a moment all he was thinking of was how to stay invisible. He hunched down and hoped his feet didn't show at the bottom of the thing—he was pretty sure the crossbeams hid them, but he couldn't be positive.

He looked up at the back of the wheel and realized that if he leaned forward just right, he could see everything that was going on through a hole in the wood where the rope would go to tie the victim down.

His heart fluttered like a moth bumping against a hot light as he saw the monk walk across the room and look down at Andy, who was pretending to be unconscious.

For the first time, he got a good look at the monk's face as he studied his victim. It was not a pretty sight.

His beard, which had looked white from the top of the stairs, was really greyish white and caked with an assortment of dirt and stains that he seemed to have collected over the course of time. One particularly ugly stain looked like dried blood, and it seemed to have been there for a while.

His mouth, even closed, looked skull-like, and if it were not for his revolting beard, Jake thought his grinning teeth would have shown right through the skin of his tightly-closed lips.

But his eyes frightened Jake the most. Although they shone with life, they appeared inhuman as they burned with a blue-violet intensity that was painful to look at, like staring directly into the sun.

The monk gazed at Andy now and furrowed his thin, grey brows.

"So, my little friend. I see you have worked yourself free while I was gone. Now I wonder how that could have happened?"

With sudden panic and horror, Jake noticed Melissa crouching beneath a small, wooden table on the other side of the room. Although she remained perfectly still, she was visible to anyone who looked in that direction.

"Hmmm," the monk said, checking the straps and taking a quick glance around the room. "I think we have an uninvited guest. Whoever you are, why don't you come out and I'll get you a bowl of soup?"

He scanned the room quickly, but didn't see Melissa.

"So we are shy, are we?"

Jake watched Melissa's eyes go wide as the monk looked around the room again, this time more carefully. Like a frightened rabbit, she stayed perfectly still, and he almost thought he could see the quivering of her heart.

"I suppose I could ask you what happened, my friend. But I see you are still sleeping."

Then, with sudden and unexpected violence, the monk pivoted on his heel and smashed his fist hard into Andy's ribs. Caught by surprise, Andy groaned and curled up in pain.

"Oh, so you're awake now. I could search the room, but somehow I think you know where your friend is. Maybe you'd like to lose that little finger after all."

Jake was watching Andy when Melissa broke for the stairs, knocking the table on its side, where it spilled knives and other assorted sharp objects to the floor. He didn't know whether she was trying to save Andy from being tortured, or if she actually thought she could escape, but she didn't realize she'd tipped over a virtual weapons chest until it was too late and she was already at the base of the stairs. If only she could have grabbed a knife, he thought.

For a moment, Jake thought she might outrun the old man, and while his back was turned he made his own break and scampered towards the door leading up to the monastery itself. He didn't see what happened next, but as he dived through the open doorway, he heard Melissa screaming.

"A little girl!" the monk said. "We can have some fun with you."

Jake slid behind the door and peered out, torn between the need to run away as fast as he could, and the urge to save Melissa. He almost overcame his terror and ran back to help her, but as he looked back at what was going on, he knew it was already too late. They were halfway up the stairs, and the monk had her by the ankle and was dragging her down. She fought him like a tiger, but it did no good. The madman felt no pain, not even when she landed a sharp kick squarely between his legs.

It was no use, Jake decided. There was nothing he could do here. But if he could find an escape route through the monastery, he might be able to get help and save them. Of course, one of Jake's friends was expendable to the monk now. Apparently, he only needed to keep one of them alive.

So with fear crawling up his chest, he turned away from the dungeon and crawled down the dim corridor to another set of stairs.

CHAPTER TWENTY-THREE

The sounds of Melissa's screams tore at his heart as he climbed the narrow, winding staircase leading to the monastery tower. The terrible, heart-wrenching shrieks echoed behind him as he climbed the ancient stone stairway. He felt like he was carrying a half ton sack of guilt on his back as he tried to ignore the screams. He didn't want to think about what the monk was doing to his friends as he left them behind.

He had to find a way to get them out. His getting caught wouldn't do any of them any good, and just rushing in there in a half-baked attempt to rescue them would accomplish nothing.

Gradually, the screams faded away. Unfortunately, his guilt did not.

Finally, the staircase ended at an open doorway leading to the monastery tower. He didn't know what lie ahead, but he couldn't go back now, at least not until he had some idea of what was going on, or some plan that had even a small chance of working. He looked back once, then stepped through the doorway, hoping the insane monk didn't have an army of friends waiting for him.

He found himself in a large room with stone, castle-like walls and small, slit-like windows that let in just enough light to illuminate the room with yellowish shadows. So it wasn't dark yet, he thought. He had some time. Tapestries lined the walls, colorful but faded pictures of knights in battle, Crusaders defeating Arabs in every fight. A huge rectangular table stood in the center of the room, lined by high-backed chairs, probably a couple of dozen, he guessed, without bothering to count them.

He walked over to the table and touched the heavy wood, which was cut and carved by years' worth of use. An empty soup bowl rested at one end of the table—probably the same soup bowl that Andy had been fed from before, he thought.

To the left stood a massive stone fireplace, with a small fire still burning. He wondered where the smoke went, and if anyone ever noticed it from the outside.

He walked around the room once, looking for either clues to what was going on, or a way out. A large door faced the fireplace from the opposite side of the room, and hoping that might be the exit, he hurried to the door. Without even stopping to think about what might be on the other side, he pushed it open and found himself in a smaller, darker room.

The room looked like a kitchen area, only without the modern appliances of an ordinary kitchen. The stove was an enormous black, iron thing, as were the pots and pans that filled an open cabinet. He saw another door to the right, though, and went through this passageway to a tiny alcove with a door on each side. He tried the left door first, but it was bolted securely and wouldn't budge. This was probably the door that led to the outside, which would be padlocked shut. The door on the right opened easily, though, and revealed a set of long, winding stairs that looked like they led to the top of the tower.

He had nowhere to go but up, unless he wanted to return to the dungeon. But he'd be of no more use there now than he was before. As long as he was free, there was hope. So he took a deep breath and headed up.

The steep staircase wound around itself like the spiral stairs of a lighthouse. Light shone in through the slit-like windows that were just out of his reach. He wished he could look through to the outside to get his bearings and try to figure out what time it was. Once again he mentally kicked himself for leaving his watch behind. It was still daylight—that much was sure—but the light seemed to be fading fast. At least he didn't have to use the flashlight. He still couldn't help thinking that the batteries might die at any moment.

The climb was a long, agonizing one. A door to the interior of the building opened up every couple of dozen steps or so, but he decided he would make his way straight to the top. Something told him he needed to go there, that he would find answers at the very top of the monastery's tower.

He passed four doors when his calves began to ache and then burn as if someone had lit his heels on fire and the flames were traveling up the backs of his legs. He was panting now, and by the sixth floor he had to stop and lean against the hard stone wall to catch his breath. He was sweating and his heart was pounding, but he didn't dare sit down. If he did, he might just give up and stay there until the monk came by and found him.

But he wasn't ready to go on, either. He wondered how this ancient, withered old monk could possibly climb all of these stairs without keeling over from the world's biggest heart attack. The stairs might be his weakness, he thought, and filed that bit of information away in case he might need it later.

Finally, when his breathing was almost back to normal, he decided it was time to move on. He hiked up another two flights before he finally reached what looked like the end of the line, a single wooden doorway decorated with a gold handle and hinges.

"Here we are," he whispered out loud and slowly turned the handle.

CHAPTER TWENTY-FOUR

He opened the doorway and walked into an enormous chapel. Yet he knew right away that it wasn't an ordinary chapel. Sure, it had the required crosses and crucifixes, and had a tall, pointed ceiling with stained glass sides that turned the sunlight red, yellow, and purple. But there was something sinister, something evil about this place. He couldn't explain it or put it into words, but he sensed it as soon as he stepped into the room.

The walls were made of the same castle-like stone as the rest of the tower. Tapestries hung from these walls, too, again showing scenes from what looked like the Crusades. These battle scenes were even more bloody, though. Jake examined the pictures carefully, hoping to find some answers.

Unlike the tapestries on the ground floor, these still had their bright, vivid colors. They looked almost as if they had been created yesterday. The knights all wore shiny silver armor and red crosses on their helmets. One knight had run his lance entirely through the body of his enemy, and this man's blood and insides flowed out in gross detail. Another knight had chopped his victim's head clean off, and another Crusader was braining an Arab with a mace.

Once scene in particular attracted his attention. He walked closer to study the image. The knight in this scene seemed to look out at him as he thrust his dagger into the exposed neck of his victim, only this Arab was a woman. The blood spouted from her neck like a fountain as the knight grinned. But it was the knight's eyes that attracted him—they were the very same eyes of the mad monk from the dungeon.

He stepped away from the painting and a shudder ran down his spine. This might be a chapel, but it sure wasn't a house of God's.

He studied the glass ceiling, which tinted the sunlight in bright colors. The windows also showed scenes of knights in battle, strange scenes for a church, yet somehow perfectly at home in this macabre place. One large picture took up half the ceiling, though, and this one seemed very different from the rest of the scenes. This one had an eerie, yet interesting design: three yellow heart shapes put together to form a rose. The interior of the shapes was brilliant purple, and the outside was colored deep red. The design was hauntingly beautiful, and made Jake shiver.

Only after he had stared at it for several minutes did he realize that the yellow lines formed a five pointed star, that also had a sinister look to it. And this star created a larger star-like image on the wall as it reflected the yellow light like a mirror. He watched, fascinated as the star slowly crept up the wall as the sun sunk lower on the horizon. In the middle of the day, he calculated, the star would be larger and directly in the middle of the room, on the floor. The design was a sundial, and a weird one at that.

The five pointed star disturbed him, and as he thought about it, Jake realized he'd seen it before—in one of those haunted houses his dad had taken him to last Halloween. The thing had decorated the wall, in a room full of ugly witches.

He noticed that the center of the floor was made of a single large rectangular black stone, polished smooth like a mirror. The bright yellow star would cover the stone slab at noontime, and the bright light would shine against the black surface.

Jake knew that this room was the key to what was happening here. He'd always been very good with puzzles, and figuring things out came easily to him. But he just wasn't sure how to make sense of all this. But unraveling this mystery might hold the key to saving himself and his friends.

He looked around the room again. Stone sculptures had been carved into the walls at each of the four corners. They seemed to be monsters with three faces, each face overlapping the other so the thing had, in total, four eyes, three noses, four huge devil-like horns, and three grinning mouths.

A chest-high stand with a bookrest stood just under the stained glass window of the rose. It was exactly the same kind of bookrest Father Barrett had beside the altar at St. Kevin's, where he read from an oversized Bible at mass.

He walked over to the book, expecting to find an ancient, yellowed copy of the Bible. The book was a relic, all right, and hundreds of years old by the looks of it. Yet the yellowed pages, which should have been brittle with age, felt as if they were brand new. He immediately knew that this book was not any version of the Bible that he'd ever seen. It was written in some foreign language. French. He'd studied a little bit of it in school, but was far from fluent. But he could recognize a few words here and there. "Mort." Dead. "Vie." Life. "Diable." Devil. Life and death and devils. It wasn't looking good.

A red, silk bookmark in the shape of a cross held the page, and he gently closed the book to examine the cover.

The book was bound with soft, brown leather that almost resembled skin. The rose design of the stained glass window was repeated on the cover with the same bright colors engraved into the surface. The cover had no title, so he turned to the title page to try to figure out what he was looking at. This was French too. "*Le Livre de Ordre du Temple.*" The book of the order of the temple? Unless it had something to do with the Knights Templar. He'd read about them somewhere.

This must be the book of the Knights Templar, which made sense when you looked at the pictures of the Crusaders on the walls. The knights with the red crosses on their chests and shields.

He tried to remember what he knew of the Knights Templar. He remembered that one of the characters in *Ivanhoe* was one; they were combinations of knights and monks—monks who fought the Arabs. He remembered that they'd become very rich and had gotten into trouble with the church. A few had been burned at the stake. They were somehow connected to Friday the 13th, but he couldn't remember how. They were arrested then, way back in the middle ages, he thought. But it was all fuzzy.

But as soon as he started looking through the book, he began to understand.

Although he could only understand a few of the words, he had no problem making sense of the ink drawings. Those were quite clear, and if they were any indication of what was going on in this monastery, then he and his friends were in serious trouble. The etchings were in great detail, and they showed torture, black magic, and a fiend with three faces like the ones carved into the wall. In one picture, a girl lay on a black stone like the one in the center of the room; she had a shining, five pointed star on her chest. A gruesome, three-faced monster hovered over her, drooling and slobbering in anticipation as it lowered its fierce, piranha-like jaws towards her waiting neck….

He shivered in fear. All his life he'd been told that ghosts, spooks, and monsters were make-believe, products of the imagination and not reality. Yet he did believe in the devil. And, according to what he'd learned in Sunday school, the devil did live in a hell full of demons. This monk was obviously not a man of God, but served another master. If anyone could summon a demon, Jake thought that this madman could. Regardless, he *thought* he could, and at this point that was probably just as dangerous.

As he stood there in that awful chapel and looked at the hideous, terrible picture, his entire world turned upside down. Everything he knew, or thought he knew, was gone now. This was a new reality, one where the world of make-believe had turned horrifyingly real.

Everything he'd ever seen or done seemed small and unimportant now. Any doubts he'd ever had about heaven and hell disappeared in a single instant.

And with sudden horror, he knew that unless he could stop it, either Andy or Melissa would be on that slab tonight at midnight.

CHAPTER TWENTY-FIVE

He opened the book back up to where he'd found it and took one last look around the room, wondering if he'd missed anything. He shook his head and scowled softly; he had a pretty good idea of what was going to happen tonight. He just had no idea how to stop it. He had to keep the monk from getting his friends up into this room, though. Even if the monk couldn't raise a demon, he thought he could, and he'd kill Jake's friends trying. And, as impossible as it seemed, Jake believed he actually could summon the devil.

As he thought about it he realized that this room held power. This is the place where he was strongest. Away from here, the monk was just an old man. If Jake were to challenge him, it would have to be now, while he was weak, before he had a chance to cast a spell, or summon some beast from hell. It was the only plan he had left. He had to attack the old monk now, maybe smash him over the head with the tire iron he'd been carrying around in his belt.

It was obvious that's what he'd have to do. But he was just a fourteen-year-old kid up against a guy with the power to call up monsters from hell. Who knew what else this monk could do?

He watched the five-sided star of light as it climbed higher up the wall and slowly began to fade, and Jake knew it was well after dinnertime, probably after eight o'clock. His stomach rumbled, reminding him that he hadn't eaten since lunch at Zack's house, which seemed such a long time ago.

By now, his mother and father would definitely be home from

work and would be freaking out. They'd have come looking, for sure, and Zack would have had to tell them. So they would have had to come down here searching. And knowing his mom, she would have dragged every cop and rescue worker in the state in with her.

"Then why haven't they found us?" he wondered. Something didn't add up.

Maybe they'd found the dungeon and were looking for him. Maybe his friends were already safe. Even while he stood there and wondered what to do next, his friends might be upstairs in Zack's house drinking a Coke, and the crazy monk might be behind bars, calling up his lawyer to try to get him out.

Maybe. But probably not.

Something had gone wrong. They should have found him by now. His parents would have been home for hours. Zack would have shown them the tunnel. What else could he have done? Once there, the trail would have been easy enough to follow— there were doors pried open everywhere; it wouldn't take that long to search all of the tunnels.

But it hadn't worked out that way.

Jake decided he'd better return to the dungeon and see what was going on. If his friends were still there, he'd have to try to free them. The thought of seeing Melissa lying on that slab made him want to throw up. He'd never be able to live with himself if he let that happen without a fight. He had to go back. Besides, it was the only way out; the monk stood between Jake and the only exit he knew of.

No, just waiting around for help to arrive wasn't such a good idea. Either help had already come, or else it wasn't coming at all, and that was that.

He had a tire iron in his belt, Andy's crucifix in his pocket, and a flashlight in his hand. Not much of an arsenal, all things considered. But it was all he had. Unless he could find something more useful, it would have to do.

He left the room as the last of daylight faded, and turned his flashlight on. It was time to act.

CHAPTER TWENTY-SIX

The hike down the stairs wasn't nearly as bad as the climb up. By now, the sun no longer shined through the windows, though, which meant he had to use the flashlight. He didn't know whether the monk could find his way up here in the dark or not, but he was terrified that he'd come creeping up the stairs and spot the flashlight beam before Jake saw him. He didn't stop to think that he probably had a light of his own, either a flashlight or a torch. But he was too frightened to think of anything except what could go wrong. And he'd half convinced himself that the monk was a supernatural being that could see in the dark.

He made it back down to the bottom floor and found that the kitchen and dining room were still dark. The monk hadn't come back up and lit a torch, even though there were unlit torches on the walls. The door leading back down to the dungeon was slightly open. Jake couldn't remember if he'd left it that way or not.

He stopped and wondered if he might be able to find a weapon. He took a quick look around the room to see where the monk kept his supplies. He couldn't see anything except the black kettle on the floor beside the fireplace. That was probably what was left of the soup.

He removed the cover and, sure enough, it contained soup. It was cold now, and he wasn't about to heat it up. But he went back to the table, found Andy's bowl and spoon, and ladled some of the food into the bowl anyway. He'd need all the strength he could get. He ate quickly. It was cold and salty, with chicken, broth, and a few vegetables thrown in. It wasn't as bad as he'd thought, and he emptied the bowl.

He'd hoped to find a knife or something, but it wasn't happening. He found some forks and spoons in a drawer, but the sharpest thing he could come up with was a butter knife. He decided to stick with the tire iron.

Then he eased the door open and stepped back into the tunnel leading to the dungeon.

CHAPTER TWENTY-SEVEN

His first thought was relief that Melissa's screams had stopped. That meant the torture had ended. Or it might mean the monk had killed her, or tortured her so badly that she couldn't scream. He tried not to think about those possibilities as he made his way back to the dungeon, carefully navigating the stone steps and terrified that he'd run into the old monk with each step. All he could do now was hope and pray.

The steps seemed to lead downward forever, and his dread made the path seem even longer. Finally, though, he reached the bottom step, shut off his flashlight and flattened himself against the wall as he slid towards the doorway, hoping the monk couldn't see him from inside. Once he was at the door, he peeked around the edge and looked into the dungeon.

He didn't see the monk at first, but he immediately saw his friends. Unfortunately, there were three of them now, which explained why no adults had come looking for them. Zack must have followed them down, and he had been caught, too. They were all chained to the wall on the right, their hands fastened up over their heads and their heads slumped on their shoulders in anguish. Zack was in the middle, flanked by Melissa on the right, and Andy on the left.

Yes, that explained why Jake's parents hadn't come looking for them. Zack must have gotten tired of waiting and come down here to find them. Knowing Zack, he'd probably even cleaned up the basement, pull the mattress back over the door again, and then shut it behind him so no one would have any idea where they'd gone. They'd probably think the kids had snuck outside and disappeared in the same field where Andy had gone earlier. Jake wondered if they were outside, even now, combing the field and nearby woods, and probably searching in the Bay for their bodies. Maybe they'd think a kidnapper or pervert had come back and taken them.

Which wasn't all that far from the truth, only the kidnapper didn't come for them; they walked right into his prison. Unfortunately, no one out there knew about the network of underground tunnels.

Jake should have known that Zack would follow them, and he mentally kicked himself for not expecting it. Now that he saw Zack here, it all made sense. If they were planning to go into these tunnels, they should have all come down together— strength in numbers. Instead, they'd been picked off one by one.

But there wasn't a thing Jake could do about it now. It was always easier to look back and figure out what you should have done, he thought. Now, he had to think ahead, not behind, and he had to avoid being caught.

He peeked around the corner to check out the other side of the dungeon. Then he saw the monk. He sat at a small, wooden desk with his back facing Jake, hunched over a book—probably another book of demonic spells. Jake watched him for a moment and considered his options. He had to develop a plan.

The monk appeared totally absorbed in his work and was unaware of what was happening around him. Jake knew from watching him earlier that he kept the keys to the manacles in the pocket of his cloak. If Jake could just creep up on him and crack him over the head with the tire iron, he might be able to grab the keys and release his friends. He didn't think he'd get a better chance than this.

He glanced over at his friends again. Andy was completely unconscious. After the abuse he'd taken, he wondered if it wasn't already too late. Zack looked whiter than a freshly-made snowman. Although his eyes were wide open, they stared straight ahead and unblinking, like glass beads. He was probably in shock. The two boys definitely needed help and they needed it quickly.

Melissa's eyes were closed too, but she just seemed to be resting. Jake looked back to the monk to make sure he hadn't moved, then watched her more closely. She stirred every now and again, and peeked her eyes open. She was just pretending to be asleep, he decided, but was really studying the room, probably trying to formulate a plan of her own.

After making sure the monk wasn't looking, he peeked his head out of the doorway and waved at her to attract her attention. In just a few seconds, she noticed him and responded with a smile.

The monk stirred slightly and he ducked back into the darkness. Jake had no idea what he would do if the monk came his way, but the thought of ambushing him in the darkness crossed his mind. His dad had always taught him to avoid fights—"violence is the last resort of the incompetent"—he said, quoting from Isaac Asimov, one of his favorite science fiction writers. But Jake hungered at the thought of smashing the monk's skull wide open with the tire iron; he would not feel the least bit of guilt.

The monk didn't come for him, though. He just coughed and returned his attention back to his book.

He knew he had to act. The image of cracking the old man's skull returned in crisp detail, and he could imagine himself doing it. Yes. Not only would it feel good, but it might work. But he had to do it now.

He poked his head out again and looked at Melissa and held up his tire iron. Then he pointed to the monk and pantomimed smashing his head with the pipe. Melissa watched his little show then shook her head. He shrugged and she mouthed "no."

He knew she was afraid for him, but by now Jake was convinced this was their only chance. He might catch the monk off guard if he attacked him now. Time was running out.

He was going to brain the monk and he was going to brain him now. His mind was made up. He would do it.

CHAPTER TWENTY-EIGHT

Melissa shook her head harder as Jake crept out of the door-way and began stalking his enemy. He was afraid she'd attract the monk's attention with her movement, so he put his fingers to his lips, looked away, and ignored her. Then he concentrated on his goal—getting close enough to the monk to be able to crack his head open with the iron pipe.

As he drew closer he could see that he was reading a book and scribbling notes in the margins with an old-fashioned quill pen. This was good—he'd be concentrating. Maybe he could get close enough without being seen.

Jake dropped down to his hands and knees and, like a cat stalking a bird, he began the long, deliberate crawl towards him. He moved carefully, first a hand, then a foot so as not to disturb anything, all the while mapping out a path in his mind.

He spotted a black trunk about fifty feet away and he altered his path slightly so he could hide behind it. It seemed to take forever to reach it, and he had to constantly fight the urge to just jump up and charge, but finally, he made it. He scrunched down behind the trunk to catch his breath and plan his next move.

If he crawled any closer, he'd risk attracting the monk's atten-tion. He might be able to get away with another ten yards or so, if he were lucky—very lucky. Then he'd have to pounce.

He didn't dare look at Melissa. He could only imagine what was going on in her mind, as she watched. But he didn't have time to worry about that now. The monk might finish what he was doing any minute, and then Jake would be caught in the middle of the room with nowhere to hide, like a kid with his hands in the cookie jar.

He rose to his feet, putting one hand on the trunk for balance as he lifted the iron up to his shoulders, knowing he might have to rush forward and use it at any second. Then, slowly, carefully, he crept forward, one step at a time.

One step...two...three...then he was halfway there.

His foot scraped slightly on the floor and the monk stopped writing and seemed to cock an ear towards him.

That was Jake's cue.

Charging forward, he raised the tire iron over his head and rushed at him. The monk tried to turn in his chair to face this new disturbance, but Jake was too fast and had caught him off guard. Before the monk could quite get to his feet, he drove the tire iron down to crack the middle of his brown, oversized hood.

The timing was perfect.

The metal struck his head square in the center, and Jake felt his skull crack like a ripe pumpkin. The impact vibrated up his arms with the grim satisfaction of catching up with one of Zack's fastballs and driving it deep over the center field fence. He heard the bone crack and he felt the blood fly, but the monk didn't utter a single sound.

The madman fell forward on his desk like a statue, bloodying his book and dropping his pen to the floor. Jake was screaming like a lunatic himself as he took two steps back to look at his handiwork.

The monk was down, all right, heaped on his desk like a sack, and Jake felt joy and relief well up inside him. But before he could even begin to celebrate his victory, the monk lifted up his head and turned to face Jake.

The monk was in tough shape. Not only was his head oozing blood and brains, but his entire face and body seemed to have suffered from some kind of decay since Jake had seen him last. It was as if some horrible disease had been eating away at him, and he would drop any minute.

Instead, the monk shocked him by snapping up to his feet

with a lightning-quick movement that Jake would have thought impossible even if he hadn't just brained him with an iron pipe.

"You'll have to do better than that," the monk said. His eyes were burning with rage, as he spoke in a chilling voice that froze Jake to the floor.

Jake's mouth dropped open in horror, and then he realized why Melissa had warned him against a direct attack. This man…this *thing*…had just taken a blow that should have felled a gorilla. Even beneath the hood, Jake could see that the skull had been split wide open, and blood, gore, and skin sloughed over his forehead and down his face, staining his hood and his robe as it gushed down his neck and onto his shoulders.

He didn't even seem to realize he'd been hit.

Furious, Jake charged him again and thrust the chisel end of the tire iron deep into his chest. He felt it slide between his ribs, pulling and tearing at the flesh and organs inside until it stopped halfway in. He thrust it forward again as the blood sprayed out of his chest and onto Jake's hands and arms, then he felt something give and the iron went straight through, the end popping out on the other side, right between his shoulder blades. The movement carried Jake forward into the monk's arms. He let go of the weapon and leaped back before he could grab him and pull him in.

The tire iron had run him completely through. He staggered backward, crashing into the desk again and knocking it over. Then he stood up, stared into Jake's eyes, and laughed.

Jake watched in horror as the monk looked down at the tire iron, then slowly pulled it out. He held the dripping weapon up for his attacker to see, then tossed it on the floor as if it were just a splinter he'd removed from his little finger.

"Midnight approaches," the monk said. "Would you like to join the dance too, my little friend?"

CHAPTER TWENTY-NINE

Jake's brain went numb as he tried to understand what had just happened. The monk couldn't be still standing. But he was.

Fortunately, fear and instinct took control of his body, and though he couldn't think, he definitely could run. He didn't even realize he was running until he had passed through the doorway and found himself scurrying up the stairs towards the monastery tower, taking the treacherous steps two and three at a time.

Jake was the mouse now, and the monk was the cat running just behind him, just a fingertip away, his hot, foul-smelling breath on his back. Jake knew if he let up for even a fraction of a second, he was gone. He crashed through the partially open door and fell into the dining room, crashing into the darkness and somehow rolling between two chairs and underneath the table.

The fall saved him. The monk crashed into the room, too, only instead of falling, he smashed directly into the table and sprawled across it. He landed hard, just above Jake, who scurried to the end of the table closest to the kitchen.

He had no idea how a man so old could move so fast, especially after he had been brained with a tire iron, and then run completely through with the chisel end of the pipe. He fumbled in his pocket for the flashlight, then, once he found it he didn't dare to turn it on and give himself away. At least the thing couldn't see in the dark, Jake thought as he wormed himself between the table leg and the last chair, desperately trying to remember where the kitchen door was located. The monk swore and pushed himself off the table and, fortunately for Jake, headed towards the opposite end of the room.

He crept out along the stone floor until he found the wall, then stood up, placing his back against the bricks. He slowly felt his way along the wall until he reached the door, which he had left partly open. Then he rushed through, slammed the door shut and turned on his flashlight.

The monk heard him of course, and tripped his way across the room as Jake hurried across the kitchen and up the stairs. He had just made it to the door leading up when the cleric crashed into the kitchen and saw him. He hurried through the doorway, slammed the door shut, then raced up the stairs. He heard the monk scrambling across the kitchen, knocking things over in the darkness and cursing in fury. He heard him fall once, and then the door behind Jake flew open, yanked from its hinges. Now the monk was on the stairs, too.

"Your death will last the longest!" he shrieked.

Jake thought his voice was becoming wetter, like a teakettle boiling and bubbling over.

He realized that this monk wasn't a man at all, but some sort of undead thing that had been kept alive by spells and magic. No living thing could survive what it had. But it had kept coming.

He knew then that he couldn't outrun it. If an iron pipe went through the thing's chest with no effect, then he couldn't stop it. It was only a matter of time until he was caught.

Still, he ran as fast and hard as he could, ignoring the pain in his legs and lungs, knowing he would probably die, but not without a fight, however futile. The monked monster was closing fast, following the flashlight like a beacon as its eerie light illuminated the stairs. But if Jake shut the light off, he'd crash and fall.

He beat him to the third floor and considered opening the door and going into the monastery building. But if it were locked he'd be slowed down just enough to be caught. His lungs burned in agony as he gasped for air, but he kept going, fueled by adrenaline.

Then, just as the terrible, bony fingers touched the back of Jake's ankle, the monk screamed in anger and surprise as his feet went out from under him. Jake heard a loud thump as the monk's body struck the stairs. The crash was followed by another series of bumps as the monk slid and tumbled down the stairs, rolling all the way back to the bottom, three flights down.

Jake stopped just for a moment to shine the flashlight back. The monk was out of sight, raving in French at the bottom of the stairs. But he couldn't linger. If the tire iron hadn't hurt him, then the fall hadn't either, and he'd be back, probably as soon as he could find a torch and make some light.

He had a good head start now, and the monk wouldn't know where he'd gone. Some of the monastery doors were probably open, or he could kick them in. But he decided he was going to return to the very top of the tower. That's where the "dance" was going to happen, as the monk called it. And he planned to be there and do whatever he could to ruin the party.

CHAPTER THIRTY

Jake knew the monk's fall had bought him enough time so that he could easily beat his pursuer to the chapel at the top of the tower. Some of the doors leading into the monastery were, in fact, unlocked, he found, and he opened them as he went along, just to leave a false trail. But the chapel was his goal; whatever was about to transpire would happen there. So he trusted himself to fate, murmured a soft prayer, and hurried up the stairs. Down below, the monk fumbled around in the darkness. He'd never make it up those stairs in the dark, so Jake had a distinct advantage.

He reached the top of the stairs and entered the unholy chapel, closing the door behind him so none of his light would get through. The room was completely dark now that the sun had gone down. He waved his flashlight around, hoping to find something he'd missed before, and hoping to scope out a good hiding place. There was no way of escaping now, and he didn't see anything he could use as a weapon. Not that a weapon would have been much help, unless, maybe he came across a rocket launcher. The monk would return soon enough, with Jake's friends in tow, and Jake had no better idea of how to stop him now than he did before. If anything, he had lost what little hope he had. The image of the monk pulling that tire iron out and throwing it down was tough to deal with.

He couldn't do anything except wait until midnight. He had to hide though, in case the monk came looking for him. But at this point, why would he even bother? He had what he wanted and Jake was obviously no threat. Still, a good hiding place would give him an advantage when the dance did begin.

He had a number of choices to pick from. The best hideout would be behind a small cabinet on the opposite side of the room, where he could see the book of spells. That way he'd be hidden in the shadows if he did bring in a light, and he'd be able to see what was happening.

He scurried over to the cabinet, which stood about three feet high and had glass doors that housed an assortment of candles and vials of what appeared to be herbs, incense, and chemicals. With a sigh, he slumped down on the floor behind it, resting for the first time since he'd gone into Zack's basement that afternoon.

He checked himself over and decided he was all right. A painful bruise throbbed on his left elbow where he'd fallen under the table, and he'd lost his tire iron, but it had been just about as useless as a Nerf gun anyway, so it didn't really matter. All he had left was his flashlight, which he shut off to save the batteries.

Then he remembered one other thing: Andy's crucifix. He turned on the flashlight long enough so he could reattach the crucifix to the chain and clasp it around his neck, then put the flashlight in his pocket. The cross probably wouldn't do any good, but he thought that having it on might help save his soul, even if it couldn't save his life. He closed his eyes and mumbled another short prayer, hoping he could be heard in this ungodly house of horror.

When he opened his eyes he noticed moonlight shining through the stained glass windows of the ceiling. Since he had nothing else to do, he watched it and studied how it reflected in the glass. The sundial had become a moon dial, casting the five-sided star shape on the wall, where it slowly, almost imperceptibly, moved down toward the floor. So, the star would be on the floor at midnight, he realized, right in the center of that black slab. It looked like midnight wasn't very far away now.

Jake couldn't help but marvel at how the moonlight gave

the stained glass picture a particularly eerie look, especially the weird design that was both a rose and a five-sided star. The yellow star in the center of the design seemed even brighter and clearer in the moonlight than it did during the day. As if it had been designed that way.

He sat with his back against the wall, staring at the ceiling and thinking of how nice it would be to just close his eyes and go to sleep. Maybe this was all just a terrible nightmare, like the one he'd had about the monks in the supermarket. But his body ached in places he didn't even know he had, and his mind was so on edge that he knew this was no dream. He was afraid that if he closed his eyes, he'd never wake up. It was like watching a good movie late at night when you're supposed to be in bed but your parents forgot to tell you to turn the television off because they were probably watching a real good movie, too. And you want to stay awake so bad to watch the movie, but at the same time your eyes are so heavy and tired that they keep closing no matter how hard you try to keep them open. Then the next thing you know, it's morning and the sun is poking through your window, waking you up, and you realize that you fell asleep in the middle of the movie and Mom and Dad came in to shut the TV off and you never did get to see how the film ended.

Even as the thought passed through his mind, he realized that he was asleep. He mentally shook himself awake, forcing his eyes to open against their will. It would have been so much easier to just stay asleep; this was one horror show that he didn't want to watch.

He didn't know if he'd been out for just a few seconds, or if it had been hours. But his eyes finally focused on that single spot of light on the wall, the spot that had been shaped by the ceiling into a five-pointed star. It was getting closer to the floor now, and the perfect star shape had steadily grown larger as the full moon climbed higher in the sky.

CHAPTER THIRTY-ONE

The sounds of Melissa's screams snapped him back to reality as he finished the process of waking himself up and getting his bearings. He instinctively jumped to his feet and almost rushed out to help her. Then he realized that the monk was bringing her up here with him, that he would use her to summon that three-faced demon thing that would devour her, and unless he was very careful and very lucky, devour him as well. After seeing how the monk had survived the crowbar attack, Jake was now convinced with certainty that the monk could and would summon a demon. This was the real thing.

He crouched back down behind the cabinet, poised to fight if need be, though what good it would do, he didn't know. The monk might realize he was here, and if he found him, Jake vowed he would not go down without a battle, regardless of how useless it might be.

The screams grew louder until the door finally opened and torchlight flooded the room. Jake peeked out from behind the cabinet and watched as the monk threw Melissa through the doorway, followed her in, then took a quick look around.

He jerked himself back behind the cabinet and counted off the seconds until he heard the monk turn away, and he saw the torchlight recede. Then he peeked out again as the monk snapped the torch into a bracket on the wall right beside the book of spells.

The single torch lit the room in a shadowy, flickering light that illuminated the whole room while still keeping it in darkness.

Melissa's hands were chained together in front of her, and the monk walked over and viciously kicked her feet out from under her, knocking her hard to the floor. He flipped his hood down and off his head, and Jake saw with satisfaction the damage he'd done earlier with the tire iron. His head was cracked open and blood and brains oozed from the gaping wound. Blood still seeped from the monk's chest as well, staining both the front and back of his once-brown robe.

The monk's face also had gotten worse. The demented violet-blue eyes were still the same, reeking in hate and evil. But his beard had fallen out in clumps, and his skin hung off in rotted strips like paint peeling off an old ceiling. It had turned a disgusting shade of green in places, like mold, and he watched with disgust as a white, pearly maggot crawled from his left nostril and began chewing away at his upper lip.

The monk leaned over Melissa and stretched her out on the floor. She struggled, and he slapped her across the face, leaving a disgusting glob of rotting skin on her cheek. She sobbed softly as he pulled the keys from his pocket and unlocked her chains, then threaded them through iron rings on the floor and locked them again, pinning her down like an insect.

"You will die first," he said, gargling his words like mouth-wash. "They like the girls best. Then I will be restored and will take care of your friends. Except for the one who got away. I might save him for a while, and savor him. I know he is nearby, maybe even watching. If so, I hope he enjoys the dance. Once I am whole again, I will find him."

Jake shivered as he realized the monk was talking about him. Apparently his desperation had overcome his rage, and judging from the speed at which he was rotting away, midnight would come none too soon. Apparently, he had decided that the one who got away wasn't much of a threat, and he was probably right. Here he was about to watch his girlfriend be eaten alive by some abomination, and he still had no plan, no idea what to do. Some hero I turned out to be, Jake thought.

He could see that the five-pointed star had moved down the

wall and was creeping across the floor towards Melissa's chest. The monk looked at the star, even as Jake did, and when the monk grinned, another maggot escaped from between his lips. Then he returned to stand in front of the book of spells where it waited for him on its bookrest.

He had to keep the light from reaching her. Or keep the monk from reading the spell. It was the spell and the light, in combination. He had to stop it.

He might be able to break the stained glass window. But he didn't have anything heavy enough to throw at it, except his flashlight maybe. But that was plastic and wouldn't be strong enough. Unless he could somehow block out the light so it wouldn't touch Melissa.

Then he felt Andy's crucifix suddenly grow hot on his neck, and an idea popped into his mind. It was insane. But he was desperate.

The monk opened the book to a specific page, raised his rotting hands above him and began reciting a spell in a bubbling, liquid voice that wouldn't hold out much longer. Maybe the damage Jake had inflicted had speeded up the process, and if only he could keep the spell from happening, then the monster would rot away on its own. Maggots streamed from its mouth now as he uttered the French words and the moonlit star inched closer to Melissa. Already, the edge had reached her arm. It would just be a minute or so now.

It was time, he decided, and he leaped out from his hiding place.

CHAPTER THIRTY-TWO

He snapped Andy's tiny crucifix from the chain around his neck and held it up high in front of him like he'd seen them do in the vampire movies. He knew this thing wasn't a vampire, but he thought the sight of a cross might at least distract him.

"Hey Friar Tuck!" he called. "You forgot about me!"

The monk looked up from his book and grinned. Maggots covered his face and hands now, and he could barely stand as he stumbled towards Jake. As he'd hoped, the crucifix had enraged him—maybe he couldn't perform the spell in its presence— it lured him away from the book and he staggered forward, stretching his arms out toward Jake.

Melissa called his name, and he saw her struggling to get free.

"Don't let that light cover you," he warned.

She looked at him with puzzled eyes, and then she noticed it for the first time. It was larger now, growing and expanding with each second as it ticked into position on the stained glass, which magnified it like a telescopic lens.

"Jake, please stop him," she wailed. "I don't want to die like this."

She tried to push herself away from the star, but the chains held her fast. It was only a matter of seconds now before it had her completely in the moonbeam.

"Come get me!" he taunted the monk, stepping closer to him and waving the cross at him like bait.

He took another step, then another….Meanwhile, Jake inched

closer to Melissa.

Just as the star was about to engulf his girlfriend, Jake lunged forward and dove on top of her, holding the crucifix over his head like a mirror. He wasn't even aware of what he was doing until he had done it. It hadn't been a plan, but, he realized later, a divine intervention.

The light from the five-sided star struck the crucifix like a laser, and reflected off the gold, shiny surface and onto the center of the monk's chest. The impact must have burned him like a welding torch as it knocked him backward, smoked and sizzled, and turned him bright, cherry red. He tried to charge forward, out of its path, but the crucifix was aiming itself now, without any help from Jake at all. It popped out of his grasp and hovered in the air between the boy and Melissa, shielding them from the moonlight and burning through the monk's decayed body. Maggots rushed from the monstrosity like ants from a scalded anthill as what was left of the monk's flesh incinerated like a volcano.

Jake dived forward and grabbed the keys from the pocket of his smoking robe. The monk's body sizzled and snapped like a steak on a grill. Then Jake scurried around to unlock Melissa and pull her free of the black stone floor. Luckily, he found the right key on the first try, and just as he pulled her free, the monk stumbled forward and collapsed on the black floor underneath the hideous moonlit star. The crucifix fluttered to the side and dropped into Jake's outstretched hand.

The entire tower had begun to shake.

"Hurry!" he coaxed, yanking Melissa to her feet as a deafening roar filled the room.

Then he realized that the roar was really a voice.

"What mortal summons me!" it said, its voice echoing through the room like an explosion. "I have answered your call. Where is my sacrifice? I demand my sacrifice!"

"Come on! We've got to get out of here."

One of the stained glass windows exploded, showering pieces of glass down on them like brightly-lit confetti. Jake and

Melissa fell and rolled toward the wall and into a ball, covering their faces and heads. The building shook harder, like an earthquake, and thunder crashed in the sky. Another stained glass window exploded, leaving only the window with the five-sided star intact; now the star shone brighter than ever, illuminating the room in an eerie rainbow of color.

"I have come!" the voice boomed. "I will have my sacrifice."

The monk, still smoldering on the floor, tried to shriek as the light took on a three dimensional form. The light focused and sparkled, and each of the three hearts that made up the rose in the stained glass turned into a different pattern. Three faces formed in the design, then melded together into a single head, still with three faces that overlapped at the eyes.

The next instant, the moonlit star had become a demon, a real flesh and blood demon with three hideous purple faces in one: four yellow, snake-like eyes, three noses, and three gaping, drooling mouths filled with piranha-like teeth. The thing stood ten feet high on two elephant-like legs, and sprouted massive horns from the top of its head.

It was the same shape as the carved figures on the walls, and the terrible flesh-eating monster from the book. And now it was here in this very room. And it looked hungry.

Jake pulled Melissa towards the door as the monster clamped its jaws down on what was left of the monk's neck.

"This one is already dead!" It spat in disgust, as if it had eaten excrement. "I demand a living sacrifice!"

Then it lifted its head. Its bright, yellow eyes looked right at Jake and Melissa.

CHAPTER THIRTY-THREE

"Run!" Jake screamed, thrusting the flashlight into Melissa's hand and pushing her out the door.

The three-faced demon watched confidently, knowing Jake was no match for it. Melissa looked back at him with a mixture of regret, terror, and pride—pride in him for what he had done and what he was about to do. She hesitated and took a step back towards him.

"Go!" he screamed, and handed her the keys. "Save the others and get out. Otherwise, this thing will kill us both."

She wanted to say something, but Jake turned away from her and slammed the door shut so she couldn't come back in. With relief, he heard her scamper down the stairs and she was gone. It was just him and the demon now.

The monster looked down at the monk with disgust, then grabbed his body and threw it aside like a sack of garbage. What wasn't rotting had turned to ash, and left a trail of dust behind. Even Jake's flashlight was gone now and the torch was still in its holder at the other side of the chapel, behind the book of spells. Jake slowly circled the monster, trying to make his way to the torch and try to lure the demon away from the door to give Melissa more time to escape. Although he didn't expect a flame to have any effect on this creature from the world of fire and brimstone, he knew he'd need light if he were to have any hope of escaping from this horrible place.

"Come to me!" the demon demanded, looking directly at Jake with its middle face while the faces on either side twisted to look at him too, bringing all four yellow eyes upon him.

The eyes seemed to draw him in, to command him, and to lure him. He felt himself stop moving as he gazed back, unable to close his eyes or look away.

"Yes. Come to me. Join with me and live forever," it commanded in a soothing syrupy voice like that of a nurse before she drives the hypodermic needle home.

He felt his feet turn towards it, moving on their own without his will.

Sudden terror paralyzed his brain as he felt control of his body slip away. The demon's three drooling mouths opened in anticipation, and he felt himself moving forward as if he were being pulled on a string.

In that instant, the worst moment of his fourteen-year-old life, Jake thought it was all over. He was dead and his soul was probably lost as well. But he didn't care. At least he'd managed to save Melissa. She would get away and release his friends.

That was if the demon didn't go after her, too.

If it killed him too quickly, it might go after her, too, and the rest, for he had no doubt that this creature's appetite was immense. The spell probably kept it in check. But Jake didn't know the spell, or how it worked. The demon might even be able to remain in the real world now; it might have permanently escaped from the fiery pits of hell and was now free to roam at will and terrorize the world.

If that happened, his sacrifice was for nothing. He'd resigned himself to die, to give himself up for the greater good, but that thought jarred at his brain now, and his feet stopped moving as he imagined Melissa being caught at the bottom of the stairs, or in the dungeon.

No. He couldn't let that happen.

He felt Andy's crucifix burning against the palm of his hand where he was still clutching it. The relic had burned deep into his flesh, but he hadn't even noticed it. He opened his hand and the metal cooled instantly and he held it between his fingers. It had burned a mark into his palm, the mark of Jesus on the cross, a mark that would turn into a lifelong scar, a reminder, he thought—if he lived that long.

Jake lifted the cross in front of him once again, holding it forward like a shield, just like he'd done with the monk. But this monster, this demon, did not step towards it. It lurched back, as if it had been hit with a hot poker.

Although the cross was only an inch long, the tiny relic felt like a broadsword in his hand. Somehow he'd managed to maneuver the torchlight behind him, and its light cast an elongated shadow of the cross directly onto the demon's chest.

The demon looked down at the shadow for a moment, examining the thing like a baby might do when given a brand new toy. Then its fascination vanished as the cross began to burn its image onto the monster's flesh. It's eyes bugged out in horror, all four of them, as it experienced pain and defeat for the first time in its existence. It clutched its chest, trying desperately to make this new sensation go away, yet it could not. Then it let out a deafening screech, fouling the air with its hideous breath and the reek of burning flesh.

Still holding the cross before him, Jake backed up and grabbed the torch. The monster's hands caught fire as they fell into the shadow of the crucifix, and it backed away. Then, with a look of hatred, loathing, and agony, it unfurled a set of wings from somewhere and flew straight into the last stained glass window, the one with the rose and the five-pointed star.

With a final shriek and an explosion of colored glass, the thing was gone, transported back to its own fiendish, feverish world.

Jake looked up through the gaping hole in the ceiling and stared at the moon in the clear, night sky. Then, when he was sure it was over, he placed the torch on the dry, brittle pages of the *Book of the Knights Templar*, which still lay open on the bookrest. The ancient pages caught instantly, greedy for the flames, which fed on them well.

Once the book was engulfed, Jake sat down on the stone floor and wept until the tears would come no more.

EPILOGUE

Only a couple of dozen mourners attended Andy's funeral. Jake wasn't surprised. Most of his family was gone, and his friend had never quite fit in again, afterwards, so he hadn't made new friends and had never married. He guessed none of them had quite fit in again. They'd each dealt with it in their own way. Jake had found God. Zack and Melissa had found drugs and alcohol. And Andy...well, Andy had found peace at last.

Jake had been taught that suicide was the unpardonable, the unforgivable sin. But he believed there were mitigating circumstances. And this was one of them. So he had delivered the sermon, prayed for Andy's soul, and assured those present that, despite the tragic circumstances, Andy's soul was safe, that it looked down on them from heaven, even now. And, knowing what he knew, he believed every word of it.

Zack hadn't made the service, and Jake wasn't surprised. In fact, he was relieved. He was afraid to see what his friend had become. If Zack were back on the straight and narrow, which he doubted, Andy's funeral would only send him back to that dark place again. He'd worried about that with Melissa, too, but his fears were unfounded.

She had been there, sitting alone in the back row of the church, and then, behind the mourners at the graveside. Jake's mouth had gone dry when he'd seen her, and he'd had to take a drink from his water bottle before he could start his eulogy. She wore a conservative, black dress, and if her hair had gone grey, she'd disguised it well, as women usually did these days.

She hadn't really changed that much, and Jake could still see that fourteen-year-old girl he thought he'd fallen in love with so many years ago. She had come alone, and she looked good. He couldn't help feel a twinge of regret, and he'd silently asked God's forgiveness for it.

After the graveside service and the final prayer, Jake had lingered for a moment. The mourners left quickly, anxious to get on with their lives. He watched them go, all but Melissa, who stood alone and waited. When they were alone, she walked over to him and looked into his eyes.

"I don't know what to call you," she said with a nervous laugh. "Father Harrison…."

"Jake," he said. "I'm still Jake."

She nodded.

"It's good to see you again, Jake," she said. "Just…not like this."

"Yeah," he said. "Not like this."

She looked down at her feet.

"Are you ok?" he asked.

"Yeah. I'm ok, now. It's been tough, but I'm ok."

"I'm glad to hear that. If there's anything I can do…"

She shook her head.

"No," she said. "I just never had the chance to really thank you. Things just happened so fast after that. And you saved my life."

Jake looked away. He couldn't meet her eyes. Things had happened very fast, all right. He'd never been alone with Melissa again after that night; her parents returned early and the next thing he knew, she was back in Providence and by September they had all been scattered around the state. Nothing was ever the same again.

"I just did God's will," he said, at last. And when he finally looked up at her, she had tears in her eyes.

"Well, I'm thanking you now," she said. "You're a good man, Jake. The best man I've ever known. Thank you."

Then she kissed him fully on the lips, and smiled.

"I hope God forgives me for that," she said. "Kissing a priest."

She shrugged and Jake just stood there, open-mouthed.

"I don't think that's a sin," he said softly.

Melissa put a small envelope in his hands.

"This is from Andy," she said. "He said you should have it."

She smiled sadly, turned and walked back to her car. Jake wanted to follow her, wanted so much to go after her and take her in his arms. But he just watched her go, and he prayed to God for strength.

Once she had driven off, he opened the envelope. Andy's crucifix was inside. Jake had given it back to him after it was all over. And now it was back here, a little tarnished and in need of a cleaning, back here in the palm of his hand. He turned it over and fit the impression into his scar. It was a perfect match.

Slowly and with deliberation, he fastened the old chain around his neck.

"Thank you, my friend," he said. "May you rest in peace."

Then he walked back to his rental car. He had a flight back to Miami tonight and he was anxious to get back home.

ABOUT THE AUTHOR

A native Rhode Islander, **James Arthur Anderson** currently teaches English and literature at Johnson & Wales University's North Miami Campus at the rank of Professor. He earned his B.A. and M.A. from Rhode Island College, and his Ph.D. from the University of Rhode Island.

Dr. Anderson is the author of *The Altar*, a horror novel also set in Rhode Island, and the critical studies *The Illustrated Ray Bradbury*, and *Out of the Shadows*, all of which have been published by The Borgo Press. His poetry has appeared in literary journals published by Bryant University, Florida International University, and Texas Wesleyan University, to name just a few. His sonnet, "The Asian Market," won first place in the rhymed poetry category in the 76th annual Writer's Digest Writing Competition. He has also written articles for *Toastmaster* magazine, *Paso Fino Horse World*, *Alberta Bits*, and *Fangoria*.

When he is not writing or teaching, Jim can usually be found practicing his target shooting at the Hollywood Rifle and Pistol Club, or riding his spoiled horses in Davie, Florida with his wife Lynn.

www.ingramcontent.com/pod-product-compliance
Lightning Source LLC
Chambersburg PA
CBHW021239260626

47155CB00004BA/1216

THOSE WHO FAVOR FIRE

These stories of the weird and supernatural lead us on a guided tour through the dark places in H. P. Lovecraft's Rhode Island, ranging from the streets of Providence to a textile mill. An artist attempts to exorcise his demons by painting Providence's famous "Waterfires"; a stranger wanders College Hill in search of beauty; an old man takes a midnight ride through the East Side on his favorite horse; a book collector finds a copy of an ancient volume that belonged to Lovecraft himself; and a fisherman learns that sometimes it's just better to let that award-winning trophy get away.

A dozen tales to thrill and chill by the author of *The Altar* and *The Monastery*!

Borgo Press Books by JAMES ARTHUR ANDERSON

The Altar: A Novel of Horror
*The Illustrated Ray Bradbury: A Structuralist Reading of
Bradbury's* The Illustrated Man
The Monastery: A Novel of Horror
*Out of the Shadows: A Structuralist Approach to Understanding
the Fiction of H. P. Lovecraft*
Those Who Favor Fire and Other Horror Stories

THOSE WHO FAVOR FIRE

AND OTHER HORROR STORIES

JAMES ARTHUR

ANDERSON

THE BORGO PRESS

MMXIII

THOSE WHO FAVOR FIRE

FIRST EDITION

Published by Wildside Press LLC

www.wildsidebooks.com

DEDICATION

To My Sons, Erik and Nick—
Don't Ever Stop Dreaming!

CONTENTS

INTRODUCTION
THE BLAME GAME

I'm not positive who I should blame for this book, but my best guess is my third grade teacher, Mrs. Tatro, who made us write poetry in her class. I wasn't much of a poet back then, and I had no idea what to write about. But I did know that I hated spelling, which I consistently failed all through grade school, so I took this as an opportunity to express my displeasure. My poem on the evils of spelling certainly wasn't great literature, but apparently it must have been funny, because my teacher not only made me read it out loud to the class, but took me on a tour of every class in Norwood Avenue Elementary School and made me read it to everyone, even to the sixth graders. They all laughed and applauded, and for one day in my life, I was a celebrity. I decided it doesn't get any better than that, so I continued to write things, just for fun. Now that I look back at it, it's a good thing Mrs. Tatro had a sense of humor. In a different school and with a different teacher, a satire on spelling might have earned me detention.

Of course, Mrs. Tatro isn't the only one at fault. Edgar Allan Poe probably has to take the blame for my writing horror fiction. About a year later, in fourth grade, I stumbled on Poe's "The Telltale Heart." The story gave me nightmares, but unlike most kids, I loved being terrified out of my wits. I decided it would be fun to give other people nightmares, too, so I started writing my own scary stories.

It hasn't been an easy road, and there have been some

sensible people who have tried to stop me. My college creative writing teacher begged me to stop writing "that stuff" and to write "real literature," whatever that is. And when I was still a young instructor, my dean laughingly suggested I consider writing under a pen name. I think he was only joking…but I'm not really sure.

Of course, growing up in Rhode Island had something to do with it. It's a weird place, and not just because Lovecraft lived there. Rhode Island was the birthplace of religious freedom, and since the time of Roger Williams it has attracted rogues and misfits and rebels. Its symbol, The Independent Man, still stands atop the State House, a reminder that Rhode Islanders do their own thing. They were the first to sign the Declaration of Independence, and the last to ratify the Constitution; Rhode Island patriots didn't just dump tea into the harbor—they burned the whole damned ship in Narragansett Bay, a year and a half before the more famous revolt in Boston. And, of course, the World Fantasy Convention had its birth in Providence, and despite its small size, the state is still home to more than its fair share of outstanding fantasy writers and artists, who have served as an inspiration to me over the years.

You can also blame Barry Fain, the publisher of the *East Side Monthly*, a local Providence newspaper that has allowed me to write an annual Halloween story for them for more years than I care to admit. If it weren't for Barry's harassing me every year for a new story, I probably would have never gotten around to writing many of these tales—my deadline always comes when I'm right in the middle of planning for my fall term of teaching, but the writer in me just can't bring himself to turn down a paying gig.

My wife, Lynn, is guilty, too. After all, she not only encourages me to write this madness, but she even critiques and proofreads my manuscripts. And my employer, Johnson & Wales University, also bears some of the blame. They keep renewing my contract, despite my bad horror habit. After almost thirty

years of putting up with my writing weird fiction, you'd think they'd know better by now. Finally, Robert Reginald, my editor here at Wildside, is at fault for allowing me to put these stories all together under one roof, so to speak.

I, of course, am blameless. It's my third grade teacher's fault. Blame Poe, blame my wife, my editor, the city of Providence…. But don't blame me. I just write this stuff. If you read it and then have nightmares, then it's your own damned fault.

THE DATE FROM HELL

I guess the whole world knows about me now. Three local channels picked it up on the evening news, all of them but FOX, which was too busy covering Paris Hilton's trip to China. And I'm told it ran on CNN and MSNBC, though I wasn't able to see it. So maybe that proves that everyone does get their fifteen minutes of fame after all, even a nobody like me.

It all began when I made the horrible mistake of trying to meet a woman in a bar. I know...I know...the only kind of woman you meet in a bar is the kind of woman who goes to a bar. But, look, after forty-some years of being a virgin, I was desperate. It was Saturday night and Halloween, and I decided I was not going to stay home and hand out Milky Ways to a bunch of snot-nosed kids who just made fun of me anyway.

It's not easy being a forty-two-year-old man who's never been with a woman. Everyone still thinks I live with Mommy and Daddy, but I don't. Dad's been dead some twenty-five years now, and Mom passed on in April after being sick for ever and ever, and when she passed I thought I could finally have a life of my own. But it didn't seem to be happening for me.

I'd already tried all the usual things. I registered with an on-line dating service, joined the monthly book club at Barnes & Noble, and took a cooking class through the continuing ed. division of a local college. Hell, I even went to the local Baptist church and attended the Bible study classes for singles.

It was all a waste of time. The women were either trolls or gold-diggers. I would have taken the gold diggers, except I

didn't have enough gold so they didn't want me. And I'm embarrassed to admit that even the trolls wouldn't have anything to do with me. So I decided to try something different and go out for Halloween this year, to dress up in a costume and cruise the streets and see if I couldn't find a bar where I might get lucky.

I chose my Halloween costume carefully and for maximum effect. Since everyone thinks I'm such a goody-goody because I took care of Mom for all those years, I decided it was time for a change. So why not a fire-engine red devil costume complete with a black cape, plastic horns, and a rubber tail? Hey, maybe the thing would give me a new outlook on life and for one night at least I could be one of the bad boys that women seem to love. I put the thing on and was feeling pretty good when I went out and strolled down Thayer Street.

It's amazing how many adults actually dress up for Halloween these days, and so I fit right in. Halloween's very popular with the college kids. I saw just about every costume you could imagine: Draculas, Frankensteins, Werewolves, assorted ghosts, spooks, and zombies as well as storm troopers, a couple of Hershey's Kisses, and even a giant Q-Tip. Of course I was most attracted to the pretty young co-eds dressed in sexy pirate, vamp, and witch outfits, but I knew that all I'd be doing was looking. Still, I wandered into a bar where a party seemed to be going on and I ordered a drink, just for courage. I'd never drank before either, but now seemed like a good night to start.

It wasn't long before I spotted another devil like myself, only this one was female and looked a lot better in her costume than I did in mine. Her version of a devil costume was an ultra-tight red cat suit that clung like skin over a centerfold body. Her hair was jet-black with two red horns protruding, no doubt held in place by an unseen clip or something. And her eyes were, by contrast, emerald blue and bottomless. She was in her twenties and so far out of my league that I'd have a better chance of beating LeBron James in one-on-one than getting even the time of day from her. So when she turned and walked deliberately towards me, meeting my eyes, I figured she was about to

get after me for staring at her. But even though I thought I was about to get slapped, I still couldn't turn my eyes away. Yeah, think "deer in the headlights."

I thought I was going to die when she grabbed me by the hand, and the contrast of her butter-soft fingers with long red nails was profound to the third degree.

"Hey, want to take me to a party?" she said, looking me straight in the eye. "I need a date and our costumes match."

"Huh?"

"Besides, you're kind of cute. Want to come?"

I felt her fingers slide a tickle into my palm and I almost fainted right then and there, which, in hindsight, would have been the best thing I could have done. But somehow I managed to stay on my feet and stammer out a reply that she must have interpreted as being the "yes" I intended.

"Great," she said. Then she leaned over and kissed me right on the lips and the next thing I knew she was dragging me out of the bar and down the street.

This woman had a body to die for—of course, I didn't take that literally at the time—and here *she* was picking *me* up in a bar. Yeah, I would have followed her anywhere. And, I did. Straight to hell, in fact.

She led me through a maze of dark streets until we came to an old house somewhere behind Benefit Street, I think. It was dark and getting cold but I didn't care. I was so excited that I generated my own heat.

Once I got my breath back, I started thinking that this was just too good to be true. It must be some kind of practical joke. But I didn't know anyone well enough for them to even play a joke on me.

"What's your name?" she asked as we stopped at the door of the house.

"Stevie."

"That's a sexy name." She squeezed my hand. Then she told me her name but somehow the wind took it and I couldn't hear, and before I could ask her to repeat it the door had opened and

she'd whisked me through, into a large room lit with candles that flickered against themselves. Then I noticed that the walls were all mirrors. And the floor seemed to be clear glass.

We were the only ones in the room, which was just fine by me, and she led me over to a pile of pillows and sat me down. Then she snuggled up beside me.

"There, that's cozy," she said.

I felt her hand warm against my right knee.

"Very," I said.

"So, Stevie, what do you do?"

It took me a minute to remember exactly what it was that I did do. I was a computer game tester and told her so. I explained how I could work from home, and that had allowed me to take care of Mom while she was sick, and how I didn't make a lot of money, but it was enough, and how I loved playing games because I could be someone other than myself and I didn't have to deal with people.

"Don't you like yourself?" she asked.

"Not very much," I admitted.

"That's too bad," she said. "Because I like you."

She wrapped her arms around me and suddenly the thought struck me that she must be a prostitute, though I didn't think prostitutes were this pretty unless they had very high-scale clients, which I certainly was not. I braced myself for the proposition, which I knew I wouldn't be able to afford anyway.

But she didn't say anything, and for a few moments of brief but intense paradise, I drowned myself in her embrace. It was everything that heaven should be, innocent and sensual at the same time. I wished it could last forever. But nothing this good ever does.

"You've been so good all your life," she said. "Just once would you like to be bad?"

I tried to laugh, but I think it came out as more of a grunt, and she didn't reply.

"What do you mean, be bad?"

"Be bad. Evil. Wicked. You've never done that, have you?"

"Well, once when I was just a kid my best friend and I threw brownies at Mom's cuckoo clock. We were trying to hit the little bird when he came out."

"Was it fun?"

I thought about it for a moment, and relived the experience.

"The most fun I've ever had in my life. Until right now. But the next day when Mom found out I got a beating. That wasn't so much fun."

She shook her head.

"Let's do something really bad," she said.

"Like what?"

I knew what I had in mind, but I was way too shy to ask.

She reached under the pillow and pulled out a pistol, which she held in the candlelight.

"A random act of violence," she said.

I recoiled as if from a snake, but she reached over and pulled me back.

"And then, afterward, we'll come back here and you can have me for as long as you want. I'll let you do anything.... Anything."

I saw a flash of tongue in the candlelight. Everything around me seemed to be spinning, probably from the drink I'd had in the bar. I wasn't used to alcohol. Or to beautiful women.

"It'll be easy," she cooed, slipping the pistol into my hand. "We'll just go out into the crowd. Pick someone out. Anyone. Maybe someone who looks at you the wrong way. Maybe someone who doesn't give you respect. Maybe a girl who thinks she's too good for you. Maybe just someone at random, for no reason at all. It'd be fun. It would be bad. And I like boys who are bad."

There was that flash of tongue again.

"Haven't you always wanted to be bad?"

"Maybe just a little," I whispered.

Then I found myself back out on Thayer Street holding a gun under my cape, a black boxy gun that seemed to be made mostly of plastic. It was very easy to use, she said. Just like a

video remote. It was all loaded, cocked and ready to go. All I had to do was point and shoot. Just like in some of the video games I play. Then blend into the crowd, slip away, and back to the house. She'd be right there with me and no one would ever suspect. I had no motive. And I'd always been a good boy. No one would ever know it was me.

Her perfume made my head spin. In fact, I had always wanted to be bad. But I never had the nerve. I never had the guts. Until now. I could do this. I could be bad. And then I'd finally get the girl.

I took the lead now, holding the gun under my cape in my right hand, with her close at my side to the left. We walked like lovers, arm in arm, and for the first time in my life I felt like I was somebody, that I was in control. Who would it be? Who would I shoot? I looked through the crowd and picked out faces. It was like a video game. The drunken frat boy spending his Daddy's money. It could be you. The blonde cheerleader type who would put her nose up at me in the daylight. It could be you. The art student with the weird hair. Maybe you.

But no. I had something better. A random act of violence, she'd said. So random it would be. I pulled the gun out from my cape, keeping it in the shadows of darkness. Then I closed my eyes and began to shoot.

What followed was mostly a blur. I didn't realize how loud it would be. Or how many shots it would hold. I kept pulling the trigger again and again and it kept on shooting, blasting away into a crowd that I couldn't see through my tightly closed eyes. The thing held eighteen bullets. I didn't know they held that many. And, amazingly, seventeen of them found their mark, but I didn't know that at the time either. I think I set some kind of a local record, eight killed and another nine wounded and I wasn't even aiming. Hell, my eyes were closed for God's sake!

Anyway, like I said, it was all a blur of noise and then I felt her pulling me away and my ears were ringing and we were running. Everyone was running, only we had a place to go and they didn't. They just ran blindly. I was running for paradise.

It was an adrenaline rush like you wouldn't believe, and I felt like laughing, shouting, cheering even. But I stayed quiet and just ran. I didn't want to screw this up and get caught, not now that I finally had the girl.

And then, somehow, we were back in that weird, surreal house with the candles and the glass floor that looked down into a bottomless basement or something. But who cared about the house? I had the girl and she was standing there before me with a wicked smile, a wet tongue, and eyes that were like drowning pools. I wasn't shy anymore. I was brave, I was cool, I was one of the bad boys that women love, that women will do anything for. I was, finally, somebody.

"You said I could...."

"Have anything," she finished. "And I always keep my promises."

With an elaborate, exaggerated slowness, she stripped off the red catsuit and stood there before me, naked and with a come-and-get-me smile.

My jaw hung open, speechless. It was like watching a real bad car wreck on I95, one with bodies and blood and brains on the road. You don't want to look, you don't want to look, you don't want to look but you just can't look away.

The young, gorgeous body that had so transfixed me had, in a heartbeat, withered into a hundred pound prune. The hair, once black, had gone white, and the tongue, so soft, had forked, like a snake's. The eyes had turned black, cold and pitiless. The teeth had become fangs, the fingers had become claws, the horns were real and long and sharp. Her skin had turned olive green and her breasts sagged like sacks of rotting oats being chewed by maggots and everything smelled like an animal that had died some days ago.

"You can have me for as long as you'd like...and do anything," she slurred, and greenish spit drooled down her crusty cheek.

I must have screamed because my throat was raw for days afterward. I know I tried to shoot her, but I'd emptied the gun earlier and so it was useless—the trigger wouldn't even pull—

and so I ran and that's all I remember. They say they found me in the cemetery sitting under a tree with the gun in my mouth still trying to pull the trigger, but I couldn't make it work. It was empty, and even if I'd had another bullet I didn't know how to reload the damned thing.

So I've become a celebrity of sorts, though I know it will only last until the next sensation hits. Already the reporters have stopped coming, and since I've pled guilty there won't be a trial to cover. I'll just rot in prison until I die and meet my girlfriend again in hell. Yeah, that's something to look forward to.

I still get mail, though, quite a bit of it from women who want to meet me. Some have sent money, locks of hair, even naked pictures of themselves. One wants to marry me, even though we've never met, except through letters. She's real pretty, too, and I keep her picture on the wall of my cell. I don't think she would have been interested in me a few weeks ago, but now it's all different. Strange, isn't it, how the bad boys get the girls.

THE BELFRY

It was late afternoon when the blue Pontiac pulled into the deserted parking lot of the Dodgeville Dye Works. The ancient towers and belfries of the mill cast long shadows over the sleepy town. Dave Walsh yawned as he climbed from the passenger's seat and looked at the building.

It was a typical textile mill. The building must have been two centuries old. Its sprawling brick walls were crumbling away in places and the largest belfry sported a huge, gaping hole, as if it had been blown away from the inside. Dave was tired and in no mood to begin a job this late in the day. If he had been alone he would surely have left; but he knew the boss would never leave a job behind—not with the prospect of regaining an old customer at stake.

"You sure this is the place, Eddy?" he asked his boss.

"Accordin' ta the map it is," he replied. "Looks like a real dump."

"Sure does. Have you been here before?"

"Not for a while—it's been about ten years, I'd guess. The place has sure got run-down. Though it was always a dump."

Just then a watchman appeared. The man looked older than dirt.

"Who'se there?" he asked.

"We're here ta file a frame. Tenter frame number three. We're from the Winsor Company."

"Oh, yeah. The Winsor Company. The boss finisher called you earlier."

"Yeah. I'm Eddie and this is my partner Dave."

"Pleased to meet you. Name's Tom. Come on. I'll show you the frame."

They followed the old watchman through the musty corridors, past huge vats of dye and antique textile machinery.

The guard's hand was bandaged tightly from his fingers to his wrist. The gauze covering still oozed with blood and pus.

"What happened to your hand?" Eddie asked.

"Ah…nothing. I just…ah…cut it on some broken glass."

"Too bad. Hey, they still got wild cats here?"

"No, not like they used to. They still have some to chase the rats but they're not as mean. They usually stay on the second floor during the day. Just don't try to pet them. They're not your typical house cat."

"Thanks for the advice."

"The bathroom's this way," the guard said, pointing down a deserted corridor. "And there's a coffee machine upstairs. The frame's over here. It's in rough shape."

Eddie examined the chain quickly.

"I've seen worse. What is it, a ninety-footer?"

"Yup. This one's a ninety. The rest are eighty."

"Looks like we get the prize," Dave muttered.

"We won't be outta here in less than ten hours by the looks of this one," Eddy said.

Dave groaned. He's already put in an eight hour shift at the shop. They'd be lucky to finish by two in the morning. Damn this mill for calling them as such an hour! They could surely have waited until morning. And Dave did have his own work to do.

It was the curse of the times that college graduates were forced to do menial labor to earn a living, he thought. He'd been lied to. Ever since he was a child they'd told him to get an education. It was the only way to make it in the world. He'd believed them. He'd worked his way through college, struggling for his journalism degree, and then had been unable to find a job. He played at graduate school for a while, then married and took on

this lousy job with a textile machine company. The pay wasn't bad, thanks to the union, but Dave found it difficult to accept his role punching a time clock. He'd taken to freelance writing, with some success, but the sporadic checks were not enough. So he worked hard and hated every minute of it.

He opened his tool chest and prepared his files while Eddy searched for a place to set up the fluorescent lights. The security guard took his leave and continued his rounds.

Dave hated these road jobs with a passion. He'd turned down the last six in a row and it really was his turn to go. He couldn't back out this time.

"Hey buddy, ya all set?"

"Just about, Eddy. Did you get the lights hooked up?"

"Sure did. Now let's see." He took a set of files that Dave had prepared. "I'll take the far side."

The older man climbed under the frame and adjusted his light. Dave often wondered where his partner found his endless reserve of energy. He was pushing retirement age, yet didn't look a day over fifty. When Dave was exhausted from a long day's work, Eddy was ready for eight hours more.

With a sigh, Dave adjusted his own light and looked underneath the blades of the tenter chain. The blades were dulled by years of use. This would be one rough job, he thought.

"We give it fifteen rubs," Eddy said.

That meant they had to rub the file across each link of the chain fifteen times before they could even begin to file the thing. That would sharpen the blades. Since it was ninety-footer, there were over a thousand links in the chain.

In theory the machine would take a roll of cloth that was, say, two hundred inches wide and stretch it through an oven to a width of maybe two hundred and ten inches. The links on either side of the chain grabbed the cloth in their blade-like jaws and pulled, stretching it as the distance between the chains increased. Unless these blades were very sharp, the cloth would slip and not stretch, which would result in a massive jam of cloth in the machine. It was Dave's job to make sure this did not

happen.

They began their work, almost forgetting their dismal surroundings. They would file a couple dozen links, then Eddy would engage the power and move the chain forward, slowly. The finished section would move around and into the still-hot oven while the unfinished ones would emerge from the oven to be filed. They worked steadily for about three quarters of an hour while Eddy criticized the work, the management of the company, politicians, and the Boston Red Sox, in no particular order. Finally, Eddie stopped for a break.

"I'm going to the bathroom," Eddie said. "Want a coffee?"

"No thanks. I'll wait here."

"Sure. Why don't you read for a while. I'll be right back."

Dave decided to take Eddy's suggestion. He reached into his bag of belongings and took out his book. He was rereading Dracula. Looking at his surroundings in the dismal mill he wished he'd brought along something by Walt Disney.

He read a chapter, sitting in a corner of the old mill with his feet propped up on a stool. When he was done with the chapter, he put the book down; Eddy would be back any minute. In fact, he should have been back already, but he knew Eddy well enough by now. He had probably met the security guard on his way to the men's room and they were still jawing about wild cats. Then Eddy would tell him about the wonderful job the Winsor Company did manufacturing new chains, hoping the guard would say something to the boss finisher. That was how his company sold 50% of its new tenter chains, he thought.

Dave looked at his watch. It was 5:45 and already dark outside. He sat back and tried to relax, hoping Eddy would hurry up so they could get this job finished and get home before it was too late. Good thing it was Friday, Dave thought; he'd never be able to drag himself out of bed at six o'clock tomorrow. He closed his eyes for just an instant, then lost the desire to open them again. The last thing he remembered before falling asleep was the uncanny stillness of the air.

* * * * * * *

Dave awoke feeling as if he had slept for hours. He looked around; there was no sign of Eddy. He glanced at his watch. It read nine fifty three. He had slept for four hours! It was impossible. Where was Eddy? They'd never get out of here now, Dave thought.

He stood up and shook off his drowsiness. He'd better find Eddy. The frame was in the same position as when he'd fallen asleep, so Eddy hadn't returned since then. Where the Hell could he be?

He headed for the men's room. Dave vaguely remembered the directions. Making his way through the shadows and past the huge oven that housed the frame they were working on, Dave found the corridor leading to the bathroom. Perhaps Eddy had become ill. Maybe the poor wretch had passed out over the toilet or something—he might even have had a heart attack. Feeling more than a little guilty, Dave entered the men's room.

"Eddy? You in here?"

No answer.

He checked each of the stalls to be sure. They were empty, except for the usual collection of graffiti.

"Eddy?" he called, louder this time. His words echoed hollowly.

"I hope he didn't fall down the stairs or something," he said out loud.

Dave remembered Eddy asking him if he wanted a coffee. The machine was on the second floor. Dave decided he'd better go downstairs and look for Eddy, but not until he returned to his toolbox for a flashlight.

Dave retraced his steps to the frame they'd been working on. The area was still deserted. He'd hoped Eddy would be back and waiting for him. That would have been too easy, he thought, opening the toolbox and taking out the flashlight. When he even thought of venturing to the second floor of the mill, his heart pounded in protest. This would be easier if he could find the

watchman, he thought. With that in mind, he returned to the main door.

He searched a few darkened corridors before finding the guard's booth. It was encased in glass and equipped with a desk, chair, and telephone. It was unoccupied. So much for that idea, he thought. Dave scribbled a note and placed it on the desk, just in case the guard returned.

He decided to check out the rest of the bottom floor before going upstairs. Maybe he would find the guard after all. The main corridors were dimly-lit—the smaller ones were completely dark. The flashlight barely pierced the blackness between the machinery.

Dave searched quickly but thoroughly. When he passed the far end of the machine they'd been working on, he checked the spaces between it and the other frames just in case Eddy had fallen on his way back. There was nothing.

The place was chilly now that the sun had set, and the surroundings looked more bleak than ever. Just as he turned away from the tenter frame it came to life and the chain began to move. He heard the distinct crash of the fluorescent lights breaking ninety feet away.

"Eddy!" he called. "Where the hell are you?"

Dave ran to the far end of the frame, fully expecting to see Eddy moving the chain. When he arrived, there was no one in sight. The oven switched on with a roar and spit hot air from either end while the chain gained speed. The lights, which had been resting on the chain, had crashed to the floor and shattered into a thousand pieces.

"Oh my God!" Dave said out loud. He wrote about the supernatural but didn't actually believe in such nonsense. The security guard must have hit the "on" switch by mistake. Either that or there was a short in the wiring. Dave climbed over the toolbox and shut the thing off with a curse.

Now the lights were ruined and there was still no sign of Eddy.

Gathering his nerves together as best as he could, Dave set off

in the direction of the men's room again. Eddy must be upstairs.

Swallowing hard, Dave entered the dark corridor leading to the farthest side of the mill. He was still a bit shook up about the machine coming on by itself. It must have been a short. Electricity did some strange things at times, he thought.

Dave carefully followed the flashlight beam as it traced its path over the ancient floorboards. The worn oak actually bent with his weight as he walked over it. Dave passed roll upon roll of cloth, hundreds of yards of fabric in various stages of finishing. Mice scurried before his light and hid between the mountains of cloth.

After what seemed like hours of following the same endless corridor, Dave ran into a dead end. A steep flight of stairs led upwards, toward an open trap door in the ceiling. A dim light shone from this opening.

He had searched the entire bottom floor. Though he loathed the thought of going upstairs, there was nothing else to do. Slowly and very carefully he climbed the steep staircase. The flimsy railing shook unsteadily with every step.

Dave swore to himself and wished Eddy had left him the keys to the car. He'd just get the hell out of this Godawful mill and leave Eddy to his own devices. The thought of spending the night in this hellhole was too much.

He peeked his head through the trapdoor and flashed his light into the shadows. Several large rats scattered at the beam. He waited until the rats were gone before climbing the stairway and onto the second floor. He wished he had a gun, or even a knife, but how was he to know he'd need a weapon to do a routine job in a textile mill? At any rate, he didn't like the look of the rats.

"Well," he thought. "This'll make a great story if I ever get out of this dump."

He stood still for a moment and allowed himself a leisurely view of the place. The second floor was much like the first; if anything, it was even more dismal. The floorboards were certainly weaker and the lighting was worse. Spare parts littered the area. He recognized several chains, a couple of dismantled

ovens, some tenter rails, and several boxes of gears, drive shafts and motors. The chemical smell was gone, replaced by the overwhelming stench of the rats. An occasional light was turned on full. The remaining overhead lights refused to respond to any switch that Dave pressed.

There was only one direction to walk—a blank wall stared at his rear. Slowly he pressed forward, wishing he was home with his wife, sharing a nice warm cup of tea, and then a nice warm bed....

His watch read eleven o'clock. Instead of being almost finished with the frame, they'd hardly begun.

There were fewer lights as Dave continued his search. He stopped at a crate of spare parts and examined them carefully. He salvaged an iron pipe from the pile and hefted its weight. It would do.

Rats scattered before him as he continued and Dave felt a shudder run up his spine. He prayed that the rodents were well-fed.

He turned a corner and followed the corridor between shoulder-high rolls or rat-eaten fabric. Straight ahead, his light sparkled off a pair of bright green eyes.

Dave squinted into the shadows. It was a cat.

The thing was exceptionally large, but what it lacked in size it more than made up for in rancor. It snarled and advanced toward him, stalking him confidently. Dave backed away and almost tripped on some gear casings. He crouched low and hefted the pipe again, waiting for the animal to spring. He did not wait long.

The cat vaulted through the air with an angry yowl, its razor-sharp claws bared and aimed at Dave's exposed neck. Self-preservation took control. Without thinking, Dave raised the pipe and swung it like a baseball bat. He felt the impact and heard the distinct crack of breaking bones. The cat screamed, an angry, painful scream that echoed through the old mill like the devil himself. Dave felt the skull split and he turned his lips up in a bestial grin. It was the ultimate joy of conquest, of taking

the life of a hated foe, and the cat fell away from the pipe and crashed into a roll of cloth. Dave smashed it again, crushing the head into a bloody pulp. In death, the animal looked like a harmless kitten.

Dave brushed the dust from his clothes but the cat blood would not come out. He wished he could turn around and leave this place behind, leave Eddy and this cursed job to the rats. But no. It was too late now. He'd come this far and he'd see the thing through, even if he had to battle more of the cats. His confidence increased by his victory, he finished his search of the second floor, grimly clutching his blood-stained pipe until his knuckles turned white.

When he reached the farthest end of the building he found another stairway. It led to the third floor.

He had no choice now. He ascended the stairs, wondering if Eddy waited for him, even now, on the first floor. It was too good to be true, he thought, and continued on his way.

Several drops of fresh blood stained the staircase ahead.

The stairs were steep and, like the first set, they were covered by a trap door at the ceiling. The door was shut.

Dave climbed the stairs slowly and held onto the weak railings for his very life. Carefully he pushed against the overhead door. It opened with a groan, as if it had been closed for years.

There was virtually no light on the third floor. Dave followed the trail of blood with his flashlight. Overhead he heard the squawk and squeak of hundreds of bats. When he looked up at the ceiling he could see the yellow glow of their malevolent eyes.

He shuddered and tried to think of something else. He dared not shine the light upwards, for that would only set the rodents flying. As frightening as the glowing eyes were hanging from the rafters, Dave preferred them on the ceiling to flying about.

The trail of blood was sporadic but easy to follow. Dave ignored several abandoned machines of all types and stopped at another staircase. This set of stairs was long and spiral. Dave shone his light upward along the length, frightening the bats to

flight as he did so. He ducked and covered his head as the repulsive creatures flew past, their leathery wings brushing against his naked arms. Dave swallowed bile and remained still until they settled down.

Once the commotion had stopped, Dave raised the light again. The stairway spiraled upward—to the tallest belfry that he'd noticed from the outside. He couldn't imagine himself climbing those stairs. Yet the trail of blood—fresh blood—led to this tower, the one that seemed to have been blown apart from the inside. Eddy might be up there hurt, or even dying, for all he knew. The man had always treated Dave right, often listening to his dreams and plans as they rode home after a long day's work. Eddy never made him work too hard, and always treated him to expensive meals at the company's expense whenever they were working on the road. Dave could never live with himself if anything happened to Eddy because of him. Right now, he was responsible for his boss.

Cursing himself for his conscience, Dave climbed the stairs to the belfry.

The wood creaked with each step. Suddenly it gave; his foot crashed through the rotten wood and his ankle twisted painfully. Dave moaned but managed to keep from falling down the stairs. He eased himself back up, testing the injured leg. It was sore, but not seriously hurt.

When he reached the top he found a door, shut and locked before him. Kneeling on the top stair, Dave took his bloody pipe and smashed the rusted bolt. The wood splintered and the door swung open of its own accord.

Dave rubbed his injured ankle until it felt safe to put his weight on it. Taking a deep breath, he entered the upper belfry.

His flashlight did little to dent the darkness until he turned around to face the gaping hole in the wall of the belfry. Then he saw the full moon as it cast its mildewed shadows through the opening and onto the darkened chamber. Bats chatted overhead and the floor was littered with their foul droppings. It was impossible for Eddy to be here, he thought. But what of the

blood? Dave probed the darkness with his flashlight but found nothing.

Then, hanging over the edge of the gaping hole, he saw a hand. It seemed to be reaching inside, hanging onto the edge of the opening for its very life. Dave ran to it without hesitation.

"Eddy!" he called. "Hold on!"

He grabbed the hand, dropping the flashlight in his haste. He pulled. Only then did he realize the truth. The hand lifted up easily, dripping blood. The attached wrist had been severed from the arm.

Dave looked down in horror at the thing he held on to. It seemed to clutch with a grip of its own, as if it still possessed the spark of life. Fresh blood poured from the arteries of the wrist, even as he held it. Then, as he stared at it in the moonlight, unable to let go, he saw the wedding ring on the third finger. He recognized it immediately. It belonged to Eddy.

Dave forgot about his injured leg, forgot about the bats, even forgot about his flashlight as he dropped the grisly hand to the floor and ran from the tower, down the stairs and into the darkness of the third floor. He remembered the flashlight as he tripped past the machinery and debris. The bats, no longer held back by the flashlight, swooped and flew at his head.

Somehow he managed to find the stairs that led downstairs. He still clutched the pipe, swinging it overhead at the bats. He clubbed several of them before lowering himself down the staircase.

He took the stairs two at a time, breaking the railing just as he reached the floor. He continued running, disregarding any fear except that of the unknown evil in the belfry. When he finally found the last set of stairs and reached the first floor he was still breathless. Still, he did not stop until he reached the frames where he and Eddy had been working.

With his heart pounding in panic he gathered his belongings together. He left the toolbox behind and prepared to go. He thought of stopping by the security guard's booth, then decided against it. He wanted to be out of this terrible place and nothing

else mattered.

Just as he turned to leave, the tenter frame switched itself on. The oven sprang to life, bellowing out its intense heat, and the chain began moving, slowly at first, and then faster. Dave's heart pounded as he watched. He stared in horror as a new section of chain emerged from the oven. It was coated with a thin, red film of blood that was already baking into the metal.

Dave screamed in terror as Eddy's body appeared from the oven, attached to the chain. The body was baking in the intense heat, covered with dried blood. Dave's eyes were drawn to the left arm—the hand was missing.

Even as he turned and ran from the corpse he saw the security guard holding a bloody knife and smiling through twisted lips. Dave did not look back. He ran from the mill, clutching his belongings in one hand and his pipe in the other. He ran out the door and into the moonlight, passing the car without stopping. He crossed the parking lot and continued down the dirt road that led from the mill.

He saw a light in the distance. It shone from a house—part of the small mill town that surrounded the place. Once he was away from the mill, Dave paused and looked behind him. He stared with horror at the sight.

Every light in the place was turned on, every machine was running—or so it sounded—and the huge tower-like chimney billowed smoke into the face of the full moon. The cursed place had come to life.

Dave ran toward the house, leaving the terrible mill behind. When he reached the door he rapped loudly, shivering in the late October breeze while he prayed for someone to answer. Finally, after what seemed like an eternity, the door opened ever so slightly.

"Who's there?" a man's voice asked suspiciously.

"Please. I need help," Dave said. "I need a phone. Something terrible's happened."

The man opened the door a bit and studied Dave through the darkness.

"All right. Come on in. What's the matter, son?"

Dave noticed that the man held a pistol under his bathrobe.

"It's my partner. He's in the old mill. He's…he's dead."

"Dead? In the old mill? What were you doing there?"

"We were fixing a chain. They called us to fix a machine."

The man looked at Dave and frowned.

"You sure you're all right? Did you fall or something?"

"No, I'm fine. It's my partner.…"

"Son," he man said quietly. "The old mill's closed. They haven't run that place in twelve, maybe thirteen years."

"Closed! What do you mean? That's Dodgeville Dye! They called us to fix a chain!"

"No, son," he explained patiently, as if he were talking to a child. "Dodgeville Dye's down the road. They built a new mill. They closed the old one down some twelve years back when the security guard was killed there one night. They found him inside one of the ovens, his left hand missing, all cut up and burned to a crisp. I'm sorry, son. I guess I'll have to call the police."

Dave walked to the window and looked out. The old mill was completely deserted, as if it had been closed for years.

He turned and faced the man once again. He held the pistol level now, and Dave dared not move.

"Yeah, I guess you will," he said as he slowly sat down on the floor and stared at his bloodstained shirt and the bloody pipe.

MY CANINE CUTIE

It was a simple enough request— "I'm going away for the weekend and I need somebody to watch my dog. Would you be available?"

I jumped at the chance. And who wouldn't? I mean it's not every day that a beautiful blonde asks a guy like me for a favor. I was hoping I'd, like, get some favors in return, if you know what I mean.

I'd been watching her walk her dog for weeks from the balcony of my East Side apartment, and had admired her gorgeous long legs and perky smile in secret, wishing I could be the type of guy who could have a chance with her. I thought that was a joke.

Here I was, a twenty-five-year-old loser with a G.E.D. and a job in an all-night convenience store working for minimum wage, which was just about enough to feed me and pay the rent, let alone have luxuries like a cell phone, cable TV, or the internet. I was so far out of her league that I felt like a twelve-year-old trying to hit a Josh Beckett fastball. In fact, I wouldn't have spoken to her at all if I hadn't run into her in the lobby of the apartment. And I mean "run into her" literally.

She was walking in with an armload of groceries and I wasn't looking where I was going and the next thing I knew we were both on the floor laying there with our legs in the air and covered in sugar that had exploded from a broken bag, while cans of dog food and mixed vegetables rolled across the tile. I didn't know what had happened until I looked up and saw her. Again, when I say "looked up," I mean it literally. I was looking

up her dress, which had flown up to her hips, and the view was magnificent.

It was hard to turn my eyes away, but when I did I saw that she was looking right at me and knew that I'd been looking right at her. She snapped her legs shut faster than one of those giant clams you see on the nature shows, and I felt my face redden like a sunburned tourist on Miami Beach.

"Ah…geez, I'm sorry," I stammered and scrambled to my feet.

Now even the most remote chance I might have had with her was gone.

But amazingly, she just smiled that perky little smile I'd come to know from my balcony watch, and she held her hand out.

"If you're really sorry, then you'll help me up," she said.

I think the sunburned tourist went to third-degree burns now, but I somehow managed to collect myself enough to take her hand, as warm and soft as boiled butternut squash, and pull her to her feet.

Now I was looking down at her, and I do mean down, and the view from the top was as good as the one from the bottom. But I won't get into that. I watched her wipe the sugar off of her red dress and pick up a couple of cans and try to rebag them. Finally, I came to my senses and started helping out.

We got the stuff all back into the bags, all except the sugar, which was a total loss, but I told her I'd come back down with a broom and clean that up, and that I'd replace the bag of sugar.

"No, it's ok," she said about replacing the bag. "But you can take me out for coffee instead."

My jaw dropped faster than the approval rating of Congress and before I could answer, she was gone, down the hall and into her apartment, unit seven, I noticed.

I didn't even know her name. But who cares? I knew what color underwear she wore, and her bra size—34D, but I'm no expert—so I thought we already had an intimate encounter.

Hey, for me it was the closest I'd come to touching a woman under sixty since my aunt had made my cousin go with me to

the junior prom the year before I dropped out of high school in shame when I broke my arm on the parallel bars because my arms were too weak to even hold me up, and the entire cheer-leading squad was watching when I fell and they laughed the whole time, even when the EMT's were wheeling me towards the ambulance. Don't laugh. I still have a scar where the bone ripped through the skin. Needless to say, I never set foot in that school again, 4.0 GPA be damned.

I decided the best thing to do would be to replace the sugar anyway. I'd already decided she was just trying to be polite and I'd never see her again—but even that was a big thing for me. Showing up with a bag of sugar would at least give me an excuse to knock at her door and see her up close again, if nothing else. Hey, you take what you can get in life, if you know what I mean.

So when I went to work that night I remembered to bring home a five pound bag of sugar—the good stuff, not the generic brand (thank God for my employee discount)—along with the usual dried out egg muffin thing I eat for breakfast. I waited until midmorning, just before she usually walks her dog, and I went down to the first floor and knocked on her door.

She opened it immediately, and she looked stunning. Today the dress was black and shorter, hugging the tops of her thighs like a clinging child. I'm a leg-man myself; maybe you didn't know it, but now it's out there, and I was just about to go crazy. I handed her the sugar and was just about convinced she'd thank me and send me on my way. But she invited me inside instead. I could have died right then and there and died happy. Nothing like that had ever happened to me before.

"I don't even know your name," she said.

"Ah…William…," I croaked. And I mean it literally. My windpipe was so tight I croaked like an April bullfrog in a lily pond.

"What?" she asked.

I took a deep breath and tried again. "William," I said. "But my friends call me Bill."

That wasn't exactly true because I didn't have any friends,

but I was hoping she would become one.

"Ok, Bill," she said. "I'm Julie. Pleased to meet you."

Instead of the obligatory handshake she actually gave me a hug. Now I thought I had died and gone to heaven. I'll tell you, my body tingled for three days from just that touch. I knew I was hopelessly and completely in love—or maybe it was in lust, but what's the difference?

Instead of going out for coffee, she made a pot right there in her kitchen, now that she had sugar to go with it. I got to meet her dog, a friendly little black miniature poodle with the unlikely name of "Wolf," and that's when the request came up to watch her pet.

Ah, so that's the catch, I thought. She's just being nice because she needs a dog sitter. But, hey, I'm an opportunist. That hug alone was worth a year's worth of pet sitting. And if I did a good enough job, I suspected I'd get another. Hey, there might even be a kiss on the cheek for me if I played my cards right. Like I said, a guy like me has to take whatever he can get.

"I'd love to take care of Wolf," I said. "Hey, it's the least I can do after knocking you down in the lobby."

The longer I was around her, the more relaxed I became. Now that I knew her ulterior motive, it was easier for me. I knew where I fit in. I was the pet sitter. Just the pet sitter. I could live with that.

The little dog was adorable and he seemed to like me. I sat on the couch and he climbed up on my lap and went to sleep. Remarkably, Julie sat beside me. Our thighs actually touched and when she started petting the dog on my lap…well, I won't go there either.

She was going out of town in three days, and she was so grateful that she didn't have to put little Wolf in a kennel. He hated that, she said.

"And you two have already bonded," she said.

It was true. The little dog and I got along beautifully. This could turn out to be a long term relationship after all, I thought. At least between me and the dog.

She gave me a key to her place—imagine that—and said I could even stay there if I wanted, could even sleep in her bed. It was almost more than I could handle. But I reminded myself that I was just the pet sitter, and my pulse almost returned to normal. The instructions were simple: walk Wolf three times a day, as I had seen her do (I already knew the times without even being told), feed him dry food in the morning and a can at night. Change his water twice a day. What could be simpler?

Best of all, when I left she gave me another hug *and* a kiss on the cheek. I was in love/lust all over again.

I didn't see her again for the next three days—the convenience store had an emergency and put me on a double shift, for which I was grateful. The rent was due soon and I needed the cash. But I let them know that I needed my regular weekend off. I lied and told them I was visiting my Mother in Vermont. I didn't want anything to go wrong with my pet sitting duties.

The first two days were perfect, well almost. If Julie had been there with me and the dog, then they would have been perfect. But this was the next best thing. The dog was well-behaved and liked to sit either on my lap or next to me. He even slept in the bed with me, curled up on my feet. Julie had cable TV, a computer, and even satellite radio. It was like being on vacation in a five star hotel to me. She called the first day to check in and see how things were going, then said she'd be "out of pocket" as she called it, until Tuesday. She expected to be home Tuesday morning, and then I'd go back to work that night. I was in no hurry to go back to my own place, but I couldn't wait to see Julie come back. If I'd gotten a kiss on the cheek before I'd done anything, I might get kissed on the lips for doing a good job. It would be my first time. But that's just between you and me.

That's why I was so surprised when the phone rang on Sunday night, right about midnight. I knew it was her because of the caller ID, and I experienced a sudden thrill as I picked up the phone.

"Hello?" I said.

"Billy, I need you."

It was Julie. And yet it wasn't. It was her voice, but it was wrong. It was throaty and deep. Almost a growl. But it was a damned sexy growl, I'll tell you that.

"What's the matter?" I asked.

"I need you…to come and get me."

"But you're in New York," I said. "And I don't have a car."

Already my brain was trying to figure out how to get a train ticket, bus fare, anything. I'd have gone to North Korea to help this girl.

"I'm…I'm in Providence," she said. "I'm across from the courthouse. By the canal."

"You're in Providence? What happened? Did you get mugged? Should I call the police?"

I was panicked now. The girl I loved/lusted after was in real trouble!

"No. No police," she said. "Just come get me. Take me home. I need you, Bill."

"I'm on my way."

"I'll be by the statue. The one with the dead soldiers."

"I know where it is."

"Bill…."

"Yeah?"

"You may not recognize me right away. But I'll know you. I'll come to you."

I grabbed my coat and flew. I wouldn't recognize her? She must have been beaten badly, raped maybe, and I wanted to kill whoever had done this to her. But first I wanted to get to her and make her safe. I'd never felt anything like this before. Maybe I did lust after her. But this, my friend, was love.

I didn't know I could run so far without collapsing, but luckily it was mostly downhill. I just ran on adrenaline, I think, and hardly knew where I was until I saw the statue, the old war memorial. I approached it slowly, but didn't see anyone there. Just a stray dog, its yellow fur silver in the light of the full moon.

"Julie?" I called.

The dog stood up and walked towards me, its head down. It

was a mess. It had been injured pretty badly, I saw. I couldn't tell if it had been hit by a car or taken a bad fall, but it was limping and blood clotted its back.

The dog opened its mouth and spoke. It was a growl, but a sexy growl. It called my name. It told me it loved me.

I carried her all the way back up college hill and back to her home. The injuries weren't as bad as they looked and I cleaned her up, fed her some lunch meat and put her to bed.

By Tuesday morning she was herself again, the beautiful blonde co-ed I had fallen in love/lust with.

Hey, I know it isn't the perfect relationship, but it works for me—it works for both of us, actually. For about twenty-eight days out of the month, she's my best friend, her and the little dog, actually—and we can watch television, get a coffee, go to a restaurant, and have a nice Porterhouse once and a while. And if her heat cycles happen to be different from the monthly changes, which they are for ten months out of the year, she tells me, well that's a real bonus. There's no chance of her getting pregnant because her DNA's just a little off, and she is incredibly passionate when she's in heat. I won't get into details, but trust me on this one.

Now that I've moved in with her I can use my rent money for other things. And for three days or so, when the moon is full, I have two pets to take care of. I'm perfectly safe as long as I keep the fridge stocked up with raw meat and I don't let her get out to run the neighborhood. It's much better for both of us.

Having a girlfriend has made me feel so much better about myself. In fact, I've enrolled in the Community College where I'm majoring in animal science. I hope to become a veterinarian someday, and maybe figure out the science of how this thing works. It might make me famous. Who knows?

I know it seems a little off, maybe even weird. But I've never been so happy in my life. Hey, a guy like me, you gotta take whatever you can get. And what I've got…well, even for a guy like me, it's something special.

THE ONE THAT GOT AWAY

To Dan, catching fish wasn't the most important thing in life. It was the only thing. It was almost as if he had some sort of a personal vendetta against anything with fins.

I must admit, I enjoy fishing myself and don't need much of an excuse to steal away on a Saturday afternoon to my favorite fishing hole. I prefer to fish alone with only the company of the woods and the placid lake. It gives me a chance to relax, gather my thoughts, and escape from the world for a few hours. At the end of the day, when I leave for home, I usually have a painting in mind and need only an evening to make it real. I also usually leave with a good-sized trout to bring home for supper.

So I wasn't too happy when Cheryl opened her big mouth to Dan about my secret fishing spot, and I'm afraid my expression gave me away. But the awful face I made didn't discourage my brother-in-law.

"So, Larry, you've been holding out on me, huh? I didn't know you were into fishing."

I merely shrugged my shoulders and Cheryl gave me a kick under the table.

"Well," I said, giving my wife an angry look. "I'm really not much of a fisherman. I just enjoy the peace and quiet."

"Sure," Dan said. "I've heard that line before. You just don't want to tell me about your secret fishing spot. But you'll show me. You have to. I'm family now."

Inwardly, I groaned. Why Cheryl's sister had chosen to marry this character I would never understand. I didn't like him from

the very first moment I met him at the annual family picnic. He'd given me his card and tried to sell me vinyl siding for my house. I tried to tolerate him, for Diane's sake. But I never did buy the siding, even though he had been nagging me about it for over a year.

"So what do you say," Dan asked. "How about next Saturday? I'll pick you up at six."

I was about to open my big mouth and say what I really thought of the idea when I noticed Cheryl's expression. "You promised," her eyes said, reminding me that I told her I'd try to get along with Dan. I knew I'd be in trouble when I got home if I said what I really thought.

"Well…," I said.

"Great!" Dan replied. "Saturday, then. I'll see you at six. Bright and early. Got to get there before the fish wake up. The early bird catches the bass, and all that stuff."

I never could understand why one had to get up with the sun in order to go fishing. I'd done quite well by sleeping late and going off in the afternoon and was about to say so when Dan interrupted me.

"Hey, have you seen my trophy room?" he said. "If you like fishing, you'll love this. Come on down to the cellar and I'll show you what fishing is all about."

Reluctantly, I followed him, even though I knew he was going to use the opportunity to get me alone and pitch that vinyl siding again.

He led me down the cellar stairs and into his finished basement. The place looked like a rec room from the '60s with golden-orange shag carpeting and greenish-brown paneling. He led me through the main door and into a small, dark room in the corner of the basement. When he turned on the light I gasped in sudden panic. Lit by the harsh light of the single filament bulb, dozens of eyes stared back at me, expressing their hatred. I stepped back and Dan's laughter suddenly broke the spell. The creatures covering the walls were not monsters, but fish, varnished and preserved with uncanny realism.

I didn't take the time to count them, but there must have been thirty or more of the mummified fish covering the walls. Some were merely heads, such as the wide mouth bass that stared straight forward with their huge, gaping mouths hanging open at the jaws like the openings of giant caves. Others were whole, mounted sideways on boards, like the rainbow trout and the huge fifteen-pound muskeg. I stared at the grisly scene, silent and open-mouthed like the bass.

"Well, what do you think?" Dan asked. "Pretty damn good, eh? I caught 'em all myself. See. They're all labeled. Place, weight, time, tackle.... Everything. And these are just the biggest. I've got more packed away in trunks. There ain't a goddamned fish alive that I can't catch."

He gave me a good-natured slap on the back and I instinctively pulled away.

"Yeah, Saturday I'll get me another one to add to my collection. Maybe a few even."

"Don't you ever eat them?" I asked softly.

"Eat 'em? Hell no. I hate the taste of fish. I just collect them."

* * * * * * *

I was hoping it would rain on Saturday so I could get out of going fishing with Dan, but as luck would have it the weatherman predicted a beautiful summer day with temperatures in the mid-'70s. And as luck would also have it, his forecast was right on target for the first time all season.

Dan arrived at exactly ten minutes to six. I was still sipping my coffee, which was so hot it burned my tongue so that I couldn't gulp it down in one swig the way I wanted to. I'd gotten out of bed at 5:30, a full fifteen minutes before the sun, which had only now poked up over the horizon.

I grunted as I let Dan inside. He wore a white golfing hat, faded jeans, and a tan fishing vest over a red T shirt. He was wide awake and ready to go, just as I knew he would be. I hated him now more than ever.

"Hey, I see you got up after all," he said. "I thought I'd find you still sleeping."

"No, I got up," I said. "But I'll tell you Dan, I feel better in the middle of the night than at six in the morning."

"I'm a morning person myself," he said. "Go to bed at nine and get up at five. Every day. Even on the weekends. That's the only way to live."

"To each his own," I mumbled. "I'd rather stay up half the night and sleep until noon."

"Well you artists are a weird bunch anyway," he grumbled.

I gulped down my coffee, ignoring the burning in my throat. It was so early in the morning that I felt brain dead, and was thankful as hell that Dan had agreed to drive.

"Well, let's go," I said, rinsing my Van Gogh coffee mug out in the sink. I gathered my equipment—two lightweight spinning outfits, a fly rod, a tackle box, a pair of hip waders, and a small insulated bag of Bud Lite and tuna sandwiches—and followed Dan to the truck. I put my gear in the back of the pick-up beside my brother-in-law's, and hopped into the passenger's seat.

"Now, where exactly is this secret fishing spot of yours," Dan asked.

I knew that after today my secret would no longer be my own. With a sense of sadness and regret, I gave Dan directions to the secret cove I knew on Black's Pond. It was only a half hour away from the city, but it might have been in a different universe. I guided Dan along a series of dirt roads, hoping he wouldn't remember the way. Finally, we reached a familiar patch of forest.

"We get out here," I said.

Dan looked over at me, puzzled. "Here? You can't even see the water."

"The lake's that way," I said. "About half a mile."

He shrugged. "No wonder it's so secret."

We took our gear out of the truck and prepared for our trek through the woods. Dan decided to leave his cooler and three of his six rigs behind because he couldn't carry them all.

"You can share my beer and sandwiches until they're gone," I offered. "Then if we're hungry we can come back and get the rest."

"You're sure this stuff'll be safe here?"

"Absolutely. We're miles from anywhere."

He didn't seem convinced, but he didn't have much choice, either. So I led him through the dense underbrush and towards the lake.

I must admit, it seems as if we were hiking to the ends of the earth. The trail was all but imperceptible as it wound its way through the thick cluster of oak trees and tangled raspberry bushes. Dan was out of breath by the time we reached the shoreline, but even he couldn't help but be impressed with the lake.

Black's Pond was supposedly named after Richard Black, an early pioneer who'd purchased the land from the Narragansett Indians for a few pieces of wampum. But the name also fit the description, for the pond was considered to be virtually bottomless in some areas. The depth of the water made it appear black in all but the shallowest of places.

"Wow!" Dan exclaimed, scanning the pond. "This looks like a great spot. You've got your little brook entering the cove over there on the right. Your shallows over there in the little cove, and your deep water just off the rock and continuing by the overhang. And not too many trees around to snag up the line. The only thing, this pond gives me the creeps. The water's like ink. But I guess the fish don't mind."

"No," I agreed. "The fish don't mind."

"How'd you ever find this place, anyway?"

"Just by accident, actually." I explained. "I used to go hiking a lot, before Cheryl and I were married. I just happened to stumble upon it."

"I bet you could get here with the boat," Dan said, sizing up the cove. "Probably deep enough to connect to the main lake. That way you wouldn't have to walk so damn far."

"I like the walk."

"That's right. You told me you don't like fishing in a boat.

You ought to try it, though. Christ, I've got a depth finder and everything on board. You can't go wrong."

"I don't know," I said. "That takes the challenge out of it."

Dan shrugged. "I'll take a boat any day. Although I guess you really don't need one out here. But the depth finder locates the fish for you. And you wouldn't have that awful walk."

I leaned my rods up against a rock and opened my tackle box.

"What's the best bet out here?" Dan asked.

"Depends. Spinner bait's best for large mouth. Or red and white spoons. But I once caught a monster catfish out here using a crawfish."

"Catfish?" he asked. "How big?"

"About seven pounds," I said. "But they run bigger. Once I had one that snapped a twelve-pound test line. As if it were thread. I did get a good look at him, though. He was enormous. Couldn't even imaging how much he weighed, but he reminded me of something...prehistoric," I said, remembering the fish with a shudder. That was one fish I was happy not to catch.

Dan flashed me a questioning look and I knew he was wondering whether to believe me. He didn't dare not to, though, because he couldn't resist the thought of a giant cat mounted on his trophy room walls. There's probably nothing in the world more primitive-looking than a big catfish. And I think he may have recognized my fear of the fish, which only made him want to catch it all the worse. I could tell Dan wouldn't rest until he'd caught a cat.

"A big fish like that would go for live bait," he said with regret. "You didn't tell me there were big cats out here."

"I didn't know you'd be that interested," I replied. "I thought you only liked respectable fish."

"Hell, I like big fish," he said. "Don't care what kind."

"Well, you might find some crawfish out under the rocks," I suggested.

He took me up on the idea immediately, while I rigged my spinning outfit with a red and white spoon. I'd leave the cats to Dan today. I was more interested in bass.

I made my first cast while Dan busily dug at the loose rocks near the shoreline. He was soon rewarded with a wriggling, brown crawfish. He collected a half dozen of the creatures and dropped them in the bottom of his tackle box.

"There," he announced, skewering one of the crustaceans through the tail with the end of a fishhook. "I'm gonna catch me a big old catfish!"

"The best spot's off the rock," I said. "The water's muddy and deep."

"Great," he said, taking a Bud Lite from my insulated bag. "Want a beer?"

"No thanks," I said, wishing I'd brought a thermos of coffee. "It's too early."

"It's never too early," he said, and then trudged towards the large rock that formed a miniature peninsula about fifty feet on my left.

As I said, I enjoy the peace and solitude of the lake more than I really enjoy the fishing. I settled into a pleasant routine of casting the spoon, reeling it in, and casting it again. The motion became purely mechanical, allowing my mind the freedom to roam and explore. The lake took on new colors and shadows as the sun slowly climbed the horizon.

The rocks, the water, even the trees took on new and bizarre forms within the realms of my imagination. The overhang became a cliff, the distant trees became a snow-capped mountain, the tiny brook turned into a swirling river of rock and foam....

"I've got something!" Dan shouted.

His words shattered my imaginary images as a thrown rock disturbs the surface of a placid lake.

I looked over to see him reeling frantically, moving closer to the edge of the overhang in his excitement to beach his catch. From the looks of his bent rod, he hadn't caught anything worth bragging about, but from his reaction you might have thought he'd caught a whale. When he finally pulled it clear of the water, I could see he had landed a six-inch yellow perch.

Dan took the small fish off the hook, then came running back towards me. I thought he was going to ask me if I wanted the fish, but it really was too small to eat. Instead of saying anything, though, he tossed it on the ground next to the gear where it flapped wildly on the grass.

"I thought you didn't eat fish," I said as Dan plopped another crawfish onto the hook.

"I don't," he replied.

"Well I don't want him. You might as well throw him back."

"He's not yours to throw back," Dan said.

His words stopped me just as I was about to cast my line. I turned and faced him. He was looking up at me with hate in his eyes.

Now I said before that I didn't like Dan. But I'd never thought of him as evil. Foolish, perhaps. Boring, definitely. Boastful and obnoxious—that goes without saying. I never hated him. But meeting his eyes like this, I suddenly feared him.

"What are you going to do with the fish?" I asked, as innocently as I possibly could. The pathetic creature was still flapping on the ground, though with much less energy than before.

He shrugged. "Just let 'im die. He's no good."

"Oh," I said, and turned away, leaving the fish to sputter away and die as Dan rebaited his hook with hopes of landing another trophy. Simply for something to do, I pulled back my rod and prepared to cast. Just then, something broke the surface of the water ever so slightly, rippling the lake from one end of the cove to the other. I frowned. Then whatever had caused the disturbance was gone.

The incident spoiled my appetite for fishing and pretty much destroyed my reflective frame of mind. After a couple of lazy, half-hearted casts I pulled in my line and took a beer out of my insulated bag. The perch lay where Dan had left it. It was quite dead.

I pulled the tab off the beer and took a deep swallow. Dan was back on his rock, winding up with a cast that would have taken his line clear across the lake if his wasted motion could

have been channeled directly into the line. Instead, his line arched about twenty yards and then dropped into the still, deep water with an audible plop.

The sun was approaching its high point now, and though the lake should have become brighter, the opposite effect seemed to have taken place. The water was more still than I'd ever seen it, with a black, bottomless look. I gazed up at the blue sky; the high, wispy, cirrus clouds certainly were not shadowing the water. The eerie stillness brought a sudden chill, and I shuddered involuntarily. I knew that I had to get away from Dan and his catfish. In fact, if I had brought my own car I might even have packed up and left right then.

Instead I decided to put on my hip waders and do some fly fishing in the brook. I'd caught some nice-sized trout in the brackish waters before. But it was the solitude rather than the fish that attracted me most. I quietly ate a tuna sandwich and finished my beer before heading off towards the brook. I whistled to Dan and pointed to where I was going. He nodded and turned his attention back to the lake. For a moment I thought I saw another ripple break the surface of the water about fifty feet off shore, but when I looked back all trace of a disturbance was gone.

I rigged my fly line with a dry mosquito fly, edged into the water and cast my line upstream toward a couple of exposed rocks. As soon as the fly touched, a trout struck, taking it quickly under. I jerked the rod upward to set the hook and I had him.

I took my time pulling him in, feeling his power as he fought the hook. I let him run for a bit, until he headed for the rocks. Then I pulled him back toward me.

When I had him close enough, I reached down and gently pulled him from the water. It was a rainbow trout, beautifully speckled and about eight inches long. A perfect supper.

I carefully took the hook from his mouth. Then I thought about Dan and the episode with the perch. The tuna sandwich rolled around in my stomach and I couldn't help feeling guilty for what my brother-in-law had done. We had, in effect, insulted

Mother Nature.

I set the rainbow trout down in the water and released it. It drifted motionless for a moment before flicking its tail and propelling itself downstream. As soon as I let the fish go, I felt foolish. My supper swam out of sight and was gone. And releasing the fish certainly wouldn't make Dan respect the lake.

I might have argued with myself for hours on the merits of eating trout, if it wasn't for the sound of Dan calling from the lake. I would have ignored him but the calls grew more insistent, so I figured I'd better see what was going on. He's probably caught a six ounce sunfish, I thought bitterly.

I trudged upstream until I came to the edge of the lake, then I walked up on shore to see Dan struggling with something on the end of his line. His rod was bent almost in half as he feverishly reeled in the line, shouting out my name as he did so. He'd hooked a fish, all right. A big one.

I stood next to the gear and watched him as he kept shouting.

"This one's a big bastard!" he said. "Larry! Larry! I got a monster! Come on, you bastard! I'm gonna mount your ass on the wall!"

Dan stood out on the edge of the rock, perched on the end of the precipice like a vulture on a limb, looking down into the ink-black water and reeling like a madman. The line suddenly went slack and I thought he'd lost the fish; then I saw something break the surface of the water as the creature rose up to the top.

I saw only the creature's head and that was only for an instant as it broke the surface. But it was enough to know that it was no ordinary fish.

Dan knew it too. In his shock and horror, he stopped reeling and stared down into the inky depths, mouth open and eyes wide. He stood there for perhaps five seconds, suspended in time like a Norman Rockwell painting, rod tip pointed down toward the lake and back arched over the side of the precipice.

Suddenly the line went tight as the fish dove for the depths. The rock may have been slippery and Dan may have been caught unawares by the fish's sudden jerk against the line. But

I don't think it was any accident that Dan went suddenly head over heels into the deepest part of the lake. He didn't even have time to scream before he hit the water and dropped like a stone.

Dan didn't fall into Black's Pond. The fish pulled him in.

For a moment I just stood there and looked at the spot where Dan had been standing. Then the truth suddenly shocked me into moving. I ran to the edge of the lake and looked down, calling Dan's name, waiting for him to surface and swim towards the edge so I could pull him in.

He never came up. A few bubbles drifted to the surface, then stopped. Then I saw an object float slowly to the surface. It took me a moment to realize it was Dan's white hat.

I never did learn how to swim. Maybe that's why I prefer fishing from the shore to going out in a boat. But even an expert couldn't have saved Dan. He was already dead. And if they ever do find his body—which I'm sure they won't—they'll find that he didn't drown.

I saw the fish as he broke the surface, just before Dan went in. It was only for a moment, like the flicker of a flashbulb from a high-priced camera. But like the afterimage of the flashbulb, the moment stayed with me, fused forever into my brain, burned into the very core of my mind.

It was no ordinary fish that took Dan down. For in the instant that it broke the surface of the pond, I saw into its eyes and I knew.

That fish was the soul, the essence of every fish that mankind had needlessly killed, reincarnated into a single monster whose purpose was revenge. Dan had looked into the same terrible eyes that I did. And before he died, he knew.

At first they thought that I had killed Dan. They could never prove anything, though, and eventually they gave up and stopped trying, though the case has never been officially closed. They searched the lake bottom for days and never found him. Finally, they gave up on that, too.

They didn't believe the story I told them that Dan had fallen in while trying to land a fish. They knew I was lying. But they

never would have believed the truth.

I don't go to Black's Pond anymore. In fact, I've given up fishing altogether. I've taken up bird watching in my own back-yard.

I'd be happy to give you directions to the pond. It's really not very far and I think it's safe if you just follow a couple of rules. Just throw back any fish you don't intend to eat, and make sure you eat any fish you take.

In fact, it's probably better to throw back all the fish you catch. Just in case the pond gets hungry.

MANUSCRIPT FOUND IN A RARE BOOK STORE

One of the things I miss most about New England are the antiquarian bookstores, piled high with rare books, first editions, and literary treasures of all sorts just waiting to be unearthed. Over the years, I've acquired some of my most prized items in these little stores, including a first edition of *The Illustrated Man*, signed by Ray Bradbury himself; an autographed copy of Ginsberg's *Howl*, and the first Arkham House editions of my favorite author and the focus of my scholarly studies, Providence's own H. P. Lovecraft.

Transferring to a new university in Florida ten years ago put a stop to my weekly rounds in the local bookshops of Providence and nearby New England, and while I love the year-round summer of Miami, I soon learned that rare book shops are rare indeed in Florida, and what they consider old are 1960s Harlequin Romances.

However, business brings me back to the old city from time to time. When I'm there, book-hunting is always on my agenda. In fact, since my visits are less often, I treasure them all the more.

So when I was asked to travel to Providence to be involved in a documentary film project about H. P. Lovecraft, I jumped at the chance. Not only would I be able to share my expertise on the old gent from Providence, but I'd also have a chance to go book hunting. And when I called up Robert at Hidden Treasures bookstore to let him know I'd be in town, he told me he'd just

been about to call me. He had an extraordinary volume that he thought I might be interested in. But although I did my best to query him over the phone, he wouldn't give me any details until I could look at the book for myself.

Needless to say, I went nearly insane with waiting for the next two weeks, and once I took care of the rental car and settled into my hotel, I could stand it no longer. I immediately set off to see what Robert had waiting for me.

It was late in the afternoon when I arrived, and Robert was waiting behind the counter. We spoke for just a few minutes before getting down to business.

"Follow me," he said. "This isn't for just anyone's eyes."

I couldn't imagine what he had found. Maybe an unpublished Lovecraft letter, or a book from his library.

Robert just smiled slyly and led me into a back room, a room I didn't even know existed. He offered me a seat at a table and handed me a pair of white cotton gloves to put on. He opened a wall safe and put on a set of gloves of his own. He didn't say anything, but he didn't need to—his look said it all. It was the look of satisfaction, the look a big game hunter might have after bagging a wild lion. But it was also a look of worry…maybe even fear.

"I've been holding on to this," he said. "But now I'd like to be rid of it."

He placed the book on a protective sheet on the table and stepped back. I could tell at first glance that this thing was old—old beyond belief.

The binding was black leather, but not the modern bookstore leather. This looked like it had been hand-cured by an ancient craftsman. There was no title or identifying marks on the cover. I opened it to the title page.

"The Necronomicon," it said. "By Abdul Alhazed."

I felt the blood drain from my face. If I didn't know Robert so well I would have sworn this was a joke, a hoax, that I was being pranked by someone. But Robert's not that kind of guy. I looked up at him. This was a fictional book, a book invented by

H. P. Lovecraft as part of his so-called Cthulhu mythos stories. This book wasn't supposed to exist.

"It's authentic," Robert said. "Look at the inside cover."

There, in faded but legible ink, H. P. Lovecraft had written his name, and an address, 10 Barnes Street, Providence, Rhode Island, where he had lived in 1926. I noted that there was no zip code, which would have made it an obvious forgery, since zip codes weren't created until the 1960s. I recognized Lovecraft's handwriting. I'd seen it often enough at the John Hay Library while I poured through his original letters and manuscripts while writing my book about him.

"Lovecraft...owned this book," I stammered.

Robert nodded.

Very carefully, I turned the pages. It was a Latin translation, first translated by Olaus Wormius in 1228 A.D., according to Lovecraft mythology, and banned by Pope Gregory IX in 1232. Although I'm not a Latin scholar, I did acquire a reading knowledge of the dead language in graduate school and, surprisingly, the skill returned to me as I read the words.

I looked up at Robert. He knew I wanted this book. I was afraid to ask the next question, the price, because I would have paid whatever he asked, even if I had to remortgage my Miami condo to get it. This book wasn't just rare. It was impossible. It wasn't supposed to exist.

"A thousand dollars and it's yours," Robert said.

My initial shock at the existence of the book was compounded by ridiculousness of the price. A thousand dollars! This book was priceless, and could have sold for a hundred times that at auction. I pulled out the debit card and the deal was done.

I don't remember leaving the bookstore or returning to the rental car. The next thing I knew I was back in my hotel sitting on the bed with the book opened before me. Although it had been years since I'd read Latin, the language came back to me as if I'd known it all my life.

The book was arranged in verses, many of them quatrains, which made me think of Nostradamus. Some of the verses

made absolutely no sense, even though I knew I was reading them correctly. It was obvious that there was a reason Lovecraft had referred to *The Necronomicon*'s author as the "mad Arab." There were other parts that made perfect sense to anyone who was familiar with Lovecraft's cosmic horror fiction—references made to Cthulhu and Elder Gods and "The Old Ones."

Then there were spells—I call them spells for lack of a better word, but "spells" doesn't really describe these verses. There were spells to summon things, including things that we can only imagine. There were spells to make things go away. There were spells to create, spells to reanimate, and spells to destroy. And some of the spells were just beyond my comprehension. Some of the verses were immaculately beautiful, and some were obscenely grotesque. Some gave me cold chills that seeped into my very bones. None of them were ordinary or mundane. None of them can be paraphrased. For the first time I understood what Lovecraft was talking about when he wrote about "nameless things."

The book both fascinated and repelled me at the same time, but the hour grew late and I had an early morning interview with the film crew of the documentary, *Finding Lovecraft: Life Is a Hideous Thing*, and I wanted to be fresh. So with great reluctance I carefully placed the book on the dresser and forced myself to turn the light off. Remarkably, sleep came quickly.

I suffered with horrible nightmares and when my alarm clock finally went off I found myself sitting crosslegged in the middle of the room reciting a passage in fluent Latin from the book, which was open on the floor in front of me. Shivering in cold and disoriented, I was jarred into reality by the persistent buzzing of the alarm until I had to scramble to it and shut it off. I looked back at the book to the passage I had been reading.

Much of it made no sense, yet I felt that reading the passage out loud had somehow changed things. The verse contained descriptions of coldness and an abyss, and the room seemed to warm up only after I'd put the book down and closed it.

Shaken, I took a hot shower and dressed for my interview.

I met with Cat and Jim, the producers of the Lovecraft documentary, at the Rhode Island School of Design, and I talked about Lovecraft while Cat rolled the camera. The interview went very well, I think, despite the fact that I'd been so rattled that morning. I'd never suffered from sleepwalking in my life, and to wake up reading from an ancient book of spells unnerved me completely, especially when it seemed that one of the spells had actually been working. I could only imagine what might have happened if the alarm clock hadn't been set.

I desperately wanted to tell Cat and Jim about my discovery of the book, but I was afraid they'd think I was out of my mind. They had hired me as a Lovecraft scholar to comment on the literary merit of the author's work, not to rant on and on about a fictional book that actually did exist. There would be a time and a place to let the world know about the dreaded *Necronomicon*—but this wasn't it.

After the interview was finished I rushed back to my hotel, anxious to look at the book once again. I'd somehow lost memory of the passage I'd been reciting that morning, and I couldn't seem to find it again. That comforted me somewhat. The whole thing had been nothing but a dream—a very bad dream.

Still, it was with trepidation that I turned off the lights that night and tried to fall asleep. Usually my overactive mind keeps me awake until all hours of the night, and I leave the television on to watch a cable news network, hoping that will do the trick. It usually fails, but again, surprisingly, I fell asleep before midnight. If nothing else, it seemed that the book had cured my insomnia.

Once again I woke up, strictly by accident, and it was a good thing I did because, again, I sat cross-legged in the middle of the floor reciting a passage from the terrible book. If I'd gone on for even another minute, the unthinkable would have happened, for when I awoke, thanks to a sudden change in volume of the television, I felt as if I were floating in some great, freezing void, and already the walls and ceiling were beginning to peel away

and the floor was dissolving beneath me, allowing the vastness of space inside my room. Before me stood a yawning gape of nothingness, as if I were looking down into an endless well that fell completely through the earth itself. It was empty and cold, a gigantic echo of nothingness. And yet, in that nothingness there was *something*, a presence, a being that was so strange and alien as to defy description. Even its color wasn't right—it was neither black not white not any known color or combination of colors. It was beyond the visible spectrum, and yet I could see it.

The force, the power, the being—whatever it was—seemed to be calling out to me, urging me on, imploring, demanding that I finish reading the passage. It took every last speck of my will to defy that command as I clamped the book shut like a sprung trap. Only then did the room put itself back together and refocus. I looked over at the television. The news reporter was talking about the economy again. Nothing had changed. The world was as it had always been.

I wanted to dismiss the whole thing as a dream. But I could not. It had been real; it had been happening. I knew I had been summoning something. Cthulhu, perhaps. Or something worse. And it had almost gotten in. The evidence was there before my eyes. The paint on the hotel walls was peeling. The ceiling looked porous, as if there'd been a water leak. And the floor felt like foam.

I turned on every light I could find and made a pot of strong coffee. I couldn't let myself fall asleep again that night.

I'm back in Florida now, and I try to stay outside in the sun as much as I can. I've become strangely phobic about the dark. The book is stored away in my gun safe, along with an AR15, a twelve-gauge shotgun, and a Glock 34 that I hope never to have to use on myself. But it's an option if things get too bad. I don't think any of the guns, not even the twelve-gauge with half-inch slugs would work against whatever it was that I'd let in, if I wasn't vigilant and did let it in.

But for now I've been able to keep it in check, mostly because my dyslexia makes it almost impossible to open the combina-

tion safe on the first, or even second try, and so far I have woken up before it was too late. I sleep as little as possible now. The irony, though, is that I can sleep, I want to sleep, I crave sleep. My insomnia seems to be cured, but I can't let myself sleep for too long. I keep an alarm clock set for every two hours, just in case, and one time it went off just when I had actually managed to unlock the safe and was about to open it up.

I've thought of destroying the book, but I can't. I don't think it would let me anyhow. And I can't give it away or sell it. Whoever I gave it to would open the portal. I just know they would. And so now that I have this terrible knowledge, it's my responsibility to control it as best as I can.

THE HATCHLING

For ten thousand years it had rested, waiting for the stars to be just right. Now, driven by blind instinct, it emerged from its shell. It opened its amphibious eyes and sensed the world around it, sensed the emptiness, the evil, and the hunger. Quivering in fear and expectation, it reached outward with its mind, outward into the brains of the dragonfly and the frog. It found nothing. A product of cosmic forces beyond its comprehension, it coiled its snake-like body into a ball and waited deep beneath the mud where it had hatched....

The old swamp stank of death as the two brothers trudged through the muck with handkerchiefs tied tightly over their noses in outlaw fashion.

"You'll get used to it," Ken muttered to the younger boy. "After a while you won't even notice the smell."

"I hope you're right," Dennis replied.

"Course I'm right. Besides, this swamp's got the biggest bullfrogs you've ever seen. Bullfrogs this big!"

He held his hands twelve inches apart.

"Wow!" his brother gasped.

"You gonna let a little smell stop you?"

"I guess not."

"That's better. Now come on. See? It smells better already."

Dennis removed the cloth from his nose and sniffed tenta-

tively.

"It's not bad but it's still awful," he said.

"Stop whining and grow up. You'll be seven next month. Besides, you wanted to come. Just wait until you see the frogs. Then you'll forget about the smell."

The two boys continued through the thick mud and swamp grass, fighting mosquitoes with each step. A dragonfly hovered nearby and Dennis cried out.

"What's the matter now?" Ken asked with impatience.

"Sewing needle!" Dennis whimpered.

"It's harmless. Don't be a baby. You don't still believe they sew you up, do you?"

Dennis nodded slowly.

Ken sighed. "That's all crap. They won't hurt you. But I will if you don't cut it out. Now come on."

Dennis followed, keeping his distance from the hovering insect. Despite what Ken said he knew it would sew you up. It started by sewing your lips up so you couldn't scream and then....With a sudden shiver he hurried after Ken and hoped the bug wouldn't notice him.

The ground turned damp and then wet. The two boys walked through the brackish slime until their sneakers squeaked with each step.

"Mom's gonna kill us when she sees these sneaks," Dennis said thoughtfully.

"Just leave Mom to me. I'll handle everything."

Dennis shrugged nervously. He knew what that meant. He would be the one to take the blame once Ken had finished explaining. He knew his brother well enough by now to know that nothing he did would come to any good. It had been a mistake to come with him at all, he decided, but the thought of catching bullfrogs had been too exciting.

"How'd you find this place?" he asked.

"Easy. I was out looking for snakes yesterday and I followed the old swamp back into the woods. Then I found this one. It's only mud here, but it turns into water further on. Swamp's

loaded with things: turtles, tadpoles— and frogs. Biggest frogs I've ever seen."

Dennis thought about his brother's words for a moment, then spoke: "If the frogs was so big, then why didn't you catch one and bring it home?"

"Well," Ken said. "I thought I'd wait until today. Then you could come too."

Dennis frowned. Somehow he had the feeling he'd been tricked.

"But you never let me come before. How come you want me now?"

"'Cause I do. If you don't wanna come I'll take you home and we can forget the whole thing."

Dennis hesitated just a moment, but the thought of finally being able to go into the woods and catch frogs was just too much for him.

"No, no. I wanna catch frogs."

"All right, then. Be quiet. We're getting near the swamp. You don't wanna scare the frogs, do you?"

"No."

"Then be quiet and stop being a pest."

"But...if we catch a frog can I have 'im for a pet?"

"Yeah, yeah. Now just be quiet."

Dennis followed obediently as the mud thickened into a semi-solid ooze. The muck pulled him down, releasing a suction each time he pulled his feet up and stepped down again. He almost lost his sneaker before escaping the mud and climbing onto a small ridge of packed earth.

The smell was virtually gone now, and he breathed deeply of the fresh, August air. A chorus of crickets and insects filled the air and beads of sweat formed on his brow and neck. Noticing that his brother was leaving him behind, he quickened his pace, stumbling up the small hill of loose dirt and falling to his knees.

"Clumsy klutz," Ken taunted. "How'd I get stuck with a brother who can't even walk without falling down?"

"I slipped. I got mud on my sneaks."

Ken laughed. "I got mud too. I didn't slip."

"Stop teasing or I'll tell Mom," Dennis whined, tears coming to his eyes.

"Go ahead and tell Mom. Think you can find your way home?"

Dennis sobbed softly for a few seconds while Ken watched with amusement.

"Seven years old and still a baby."

"I'm not seven yet."

"Next month. I suppose you'll grow up in a month?"

Dennis dried his eyes on the front of his dirty T shirt.

"Then why'd you take me with you if I'm such a baby?"

"I thought you might grow up out here in the woods. You're always in the house all day long reading those stupid books."

"They're not stupid books. And what makes you think you're so hot? You're only ten. You're not even supposed to be down here. If Mom found out...."

"At least I don't cry and whine all the time and hang onto Mom all day long like a little baby."

"You're just jealous 'cause Mom likes me better. 'Cause you're always in trouble and getting punished. Like the time you broke the window with the ball and the time you dug up Mr. King's flower garden and the time you...."

"That's enough! If you don't knock it off I'm gonna leave you behind and you'll be lost. Come on. I wanna catch a frog."

Dennis swallowed his tears as Ken turned and slipped into the woods. He hurried to keep up but dared not speak again as they followed a tangled path leading through a patch of blackberry bushes. Dennis caught up to his brother and found him munching on the over-ripe berries. As soon as Dennis stopped, Ken ran ahead, picking his way through the thorns. The older boy carefully grabbed a particularly thorny branch, bent it backwards like a tight bow, then released it just as Dennis came near. The branch caught his brother squarely in the cheek as Ken exploded with laughter. Blood flowed freely from the painful scratch while Dennis struggled to contain his sobs.

"You didn't have to do that," he said softly.

"It was fun," Ken replied, and disappeared around a curve in the path.

Dennis hurried to keep up but, wary for another trick, could not find his brother.

"Ken? Ken! Where are you?"

He heard laughter coming from the bushes ahead. Squinting into the shadows, he saw nothing as he slowly walked forward, hating his brother with all of his soul.

Ken leaped from the bushes and ran, while Dennis chased him, panting and breathless with fear. He strained to keep his brother in sight, cutting and scratching himself on the sharp thorns as his terror of being stranded increased. He ran through the thorns, following the snaking path as if his life depended upon it. Then, unexpectedly, he emerged into a clearing of bright sunlight.

Dennis blinked until his vision returned. His brother was nowhere in sight. A large, murky swamp stretched before him at the edge of a small ridge of dry, hard-packed dirt. The brown water seemed bottomless and the willow trees on the opposite shore looked small and insignificant.

He gazed with fascination at the still water. It seemed to call him with a sweet voice, hypnotizing his weary mind. Even the awful smell was pleasant now. For a single, fleeting moment, the small boy knew peace. Then a tiny ripple on the surface disturbed his thoughts. He frowned with wonder and strained his neck forward to see.

A shout startled him as a heavy weight crashed upon his back, pulling him face-forward to the ground.

"I've got you, you little squirt!" Ken screamed, pinning him to the ground.

Dennis felt his arms being twisted painfully back and squeezed together in his brother's grip. But the pain seemed to float away from him as he thought about the stillness of the swamp, its image still frozen against the backs of his eyes. Complete stillness— all except for that one ripple.

But the stillness turned into unbearable pain as Ken released him, rolled him on his back, and punched him hard in the stomach.

"Cry baby," Ken muttered as the tears streaked down his brother's mud-blackened face, "Get up. And stop crying or I'll give you more."

Dennis obeyed. Covered with dirt, slime and tears, he crawled to his feet and wiped his eyes. Ken kicked him once more for good measure.

When his brother's fit of violence had ended, Dennis turned and looked at the swamp once again. The ripple was gone. The brackish water was as smooth as ice. Not even a water strider or mosquito disturbed its glazed surface.

"It'd be fun to throw you in the swamp and watch you drown," Ken said matter-of-factly. "I bet there's quicksand at the bottom. They'd never even find you."

"No," Dennis said, backing away. He knew his brother was capable of doing such a thing.

"Yeah, it'd be fun. I'd tell Mom you fell in and I couldn't get you out."

"Come on, Ken…," he pleaded.

"I'll think about it. Maybe I'll let you live after all."

"I wanna go home."

"No. I'm gonna get me a frog. A big frog."

Dennis followed his brother down the small hill and along the shore of the swamp, remaining just far enough back to stay out of Ken's range should he choose to punch or kick him again. They crept up a small ridge that bordered the shore and crawled under a sprawling willow tree.

Ken inched closer to the edge of the swamp; hunched behind a log, he looked intently into the water, examining its surface with expert eyes. Curious, Dennis moved closer and peered over his brother's shoulder. The water was brackish—almost black—and stiller than ice. Ken studied the swamp for a long time before he spoke.

"Shhh," he whispered. "There's a frog in the water."

"Where?"

"Next to the log. Look. See the eyes sticking out of the water?"

Dennis focused on the spot but couldn't see anything. Then, just as he was about to give up, he spotted it. The eyes blinked once. Ken was right about one thing: it was the biggest bullfrog he had ever seen.

Ken moved slowly, cautiously and reached for a fist-sized rock.

"Ain't ya gonna catch him?" Dennis asked, confused.

"Shut up and be still."

Ken lifted the rock over his head and took aim while Dennis felt the pit of his stomach drop as he realized what his brother was doing. The unsuspecting frog seemed so helpless, so unaware of death looming over its head as it sat in its swampy home waiting for a mosquito or fly to come its way.

Dennis screamed even as Ken began to move. The frog leaped into the depths of the swamp just as the rock splashed the spot where it had patiently sat, spraying both boys with foul-smelling water.

Ken turned to his brother, anger flaring his nostrils.

"I had 'im! I'd have killed 'im if you hadn't opened your big mouth!"

"I...I'm sorry," Dennis lied.

"Now I have to kill you. I'm going to throw you in the swamp and let you die."

"No, Ken. No!"

The older boy caught him by the hair. He screamed in terror as Ken punched him in the face. Then he struck out with his fists and legs to defend himself, and managed to kick Ken's legs out from under him. Both boys went down and sprawled in the mud.

Propelled by mortal terror, Dennis was the first one up. He faced the swamp while Ken struggled in the mud next to the shore.

It was then that something in the water caught his attention.

It lurked in the middle of the swamp and moved toward the shore, swimming slowly but steadily through the inky water. Although Dennis could only see the tip of the thing's nose, he knew it was much larger than a frog. He pointed to it but Ken paid no attention as he groped his way to his feet.

"I'm gonna kill you," he reaffirmed. Then he advanced toward his brother.

Dennis could see the shape in the water coming closer, drawn to him like a stray dog looking for food. He could see the flash of teeth in the sunlight, the flaring of amphibious nostrils, the glitter of serpentine yet sentient eyes....

"I'm gonna throw you in the swamp," Ken said.

Dennis tried to scream but the sound stuck in his throat. He felt the sudden rush of adrenaline race through his body and for a moment he thought the creature was inside him. In his terror he allowed his fear and hatred to take control, to overwhelm him and take possession of his soul.

With a yell he rushed at his brother, catching him by surprise and pushing him backward. The push wasn't very hard, but it was enough. Ken slipped in the mud and fell, fell into the waiting jaws that snapped him up like a kernel of popcorn.

Ken managed one scream before he was gone. Though still a hatchling, the creature was large enough to easily swallow him whole. Its stench filled the air with a burning, acrid smell as the digestive juices began to work.

Dennis watched in shock until it was done. And then the creature turned its gaze upon him.

The hatchling regarded the small boy with wonder, reading the innocence of his mind—a mind much like its own. In the other one, the one he had devoured, there had been a wickedness, a blackness that had tasted good. But this one was different.

The wickedness of the other one had satisfied him, at least for the moment. But this one could not be eaten.

Still, others would come. Perhaps this one would bring them, could be made to bring them. Or the hatchling could rise from the swamp and seek them out. There were enough others in this

world, it thought, probing the small boy's mind. Enough to feed a family of creatures. Enough to feed a planet.

And with that thought, the self-fertilization process began.

DARK SWAMP

I will begin to write, despite my trembling hands and despite that fact that I cannot possibly submit the manuscript once it is completed. The Rhode Island Review is a respected magazine dealing with factual articles and well-researched journalism. They could never publish the story I am about to relate.

Sometimes when I look back on the incidents surrounding the tale, I question my own mind. I suppose I would consider myself quite mad were it not for the photograph that is my proof. But how could I possibly ask anyone else to believe my story if I doubt it myself? Submitting the article is out of the question—that I realize—yet I must write the story, to preserve my own sanity if nothing more.

I still find it hard to believe that it all began just one short week ago. I phoned Roy, the editor of the Review, and suggested doing an article on H. P. Lovecraft, the famous Rhode Island author. I proposed to visit some of the places Lovecraft frequented and write about how these places affected his work. Roy liked the idea and told me to begin it immediately; if I finished before August 9th it would make the next issue. So I took my camera and spent the rest of the week on Benefit Street, photographing The "Shunned House" and homes where Lovecraft had lived. On Saturday I drove to Newport and photographed the old tower, where Viking seamen are believed to have landed years before Columbus.

Then I remembered hearing of a place in Chepachet, Rhode Island called the "Dark Swamp." According to local legend

it is located somewhere along Putnam Pike. As far as I knew the swamp existed only in local mythology and is supposed to be a place of impenetrable darkness where even the sun never shines. I recalled that Lovecraft had unsuccessfully tried to find the swamp, and had given up after spending most of a day in the hot August sun.

The idea of the Dark Swamp took hold of me and I was unable to dislodge it. I thought it might be interesting to follow Lovecraft's route and find out if the swamp existed at all. Perhaps there was some truth to the myth, I thought. Now that would make a story!

I packed my camera and equipment, prepared a thermos of iced tea, and put a few sandwiches in a cooler. It would probably be a long day, I thought as I left early that Sunday morning.

The traffic was light on Route 95—everyone was headed south for the beaches while I headed north—and I made good time. I turned off at Route 44 near the Statehouse, and I followed the road for a half hour as it wound its way through Providence and then through North Providence and Smithfield. I suffered in the early morning heat, wishing I'd taken the time last week to have the air conditioner fixed. I could imagine how Lovecraft must have felt, coming all this distance on a trolley and then walking for the rest of the day. I passed through the town of Chepatchet and followed the two lane road until it blended into the woodlands and rolling farms. I realized that, though much of route 44 had been built up and industrialized since Lovecraft's time, this section of Putnam Pike had remained virtually unchanged since 1923. There was no traffic to speak of and I drove slowly, taking a good look at my surroundings.

I drove by a farm and noticed a farmer setting up irrigation pipes in the cornfield. I stopped the car by the side of the road and walked through the rows of plants, savoring the sweet smell of the corn.

"Sorry," the farmer said. "I don't sell retail. The corn's for the markets. There's a stand 'bout four miles down the road, though."

"No," I said. "I'm not looking for corn. Just information."

"Oh," he said, raising his eyebrows.

"Have you ever heard of Dark Swamp?"

The farmer frowned and seemed to withdraw.

"Hmmm Dark Swamp? No. Never heard of it. There's a Great Swamp out in Narragansett. Big Indian battle there, years ago."

"No, I've been to Great Swamp. I'm looking for Dark Swamp. It's supposed to be between Chepatchet and Putnam."

"Sorry," he said, turning away quickly. "I've never heard of it."

Somehow, I was left with the distinct impression that the farmer was holding back whatever he knew.

I returned to the car and continued along the road, knowing that the swamp was nearby. I kept my eye out for another farmer or a house where I might try again for information, but all I passed was a narrow dirt driveway with a chain stretched across and a "No Trespassing" sign attached.

The scenery remained unchanged for several miles, thick deciduous forests broken only by an occasional clearing. I had not realized how far I'd come until I passed another large corn- field and then saw the vegetable stand ahead.

I slowed the car and pulled into the turnout. It was an old wooden stand, the paint peeling and the sides weather-beaten by too many New England winters. A young girl, about twelve years old, busily unpacked crates of corn and lined the ears on the shelves while an old woman sat in a rocking chair and read a romance novel.

I entered the shade and could not help but notice the fine assortment of native produce. Thinking I might have better luck if I made a purchase, I picked out a half dozen ears of corn and a few tomatoes.

The old woman carefully marked her place in the book, then bagged my purchase.

"That'll be two dollars."

I handed her a five and watched as she pocketed the bill and made change, her bony fingers sure of themselves.

"Do you know where I might find Dark Swamp?"

The old woman shuddered as she regarded me through steady eyes.

"Why do you want to know?"

"I'm a writer. I'm doing an article on the swamp."

"A writer? There was another writer who came looking for the swamp, many years ago. I was just a girl then."

"Lovecraft!" I exclaimed. "He was here! Did you meet him?"

"His name was Howard. I met him. Actually, I was quite struck with him. He looked so helpless—so sensitive. I was young and very impressionable."

"My God! You've met Lovecraft."

"Was that his name?"

"Yes. That man was Howard Phillips Lovecraft, a great writer. His books are still read today."

The woman stared into the distance for a moment, lost in thought.

"He was a most gentle man," she said. "He asked me where the Dark Swamp was."

"Did you tell him?"

"Yes. He said he'd been looking for it the week before with another man and that he'd come back alone this time. I should never have told him. But I couldn't say no."

"Why shouldn't you have told him?"

"Why? Then you don't know? I guess Howard never wrote about the Dark Swamp then."

"Well, no. He never did."

"Young man, the Dark Swamp is an evil place, better left alone. Evil beings dwell there, trapped by their own wickedness. These demons are just waiting to be let out, just waiting to escape and invade the world of men. Once I told the secret of the Dark Swamp and I have lived in fear since that day, almost sixty years of fear. I will not tell the secret again."

"Well, thank you anyway," I said, thinking she had probably read too many of Lovecraft's stories and actually believed his fiction was real. "May I take your picture?"

"Why not?"

I took a couple of photographs before walking back to the car, elated, yet disappointed. Then, waiting beside the stand was the girl I'd seen earlier.

"Meet me in the cornfield," she whispered.

I nodded, returned to the car and drove off. After traveling a little way down the road, I stopped beside the cornfield. I waited a few minutes and the girl appeared from between the rows of corn.

"I overheard you talking to Grandma," she said with a youthful smile. "I know where Dark Swamp is."

"Will you tell me?"

"Yes."

"Aren't you afraid?"

"No," she said gravely. "Grandma is old and superstitious. I don't believe in any of those stories. Dark Swamp is just that—a dark swamp."

"Have you been there?"

"No. Why would I want to go to a swamp?"

She gave me the directions, which led down the road I'd passed with the chain and the sign. From there I'd need to walk about a mile though the woods. Before setting off on foot I gulped down a couple of sandwiches and a cup of iced tea. Then, trying to control my excitement, I took out my camera and snapped a couple of pictures of the area before going in.

Half expecting a farmer to appear with a loaded shotgun, I stepped over the chain and began my walk down the deserted road. Although I'd left early, it was almost noon now and the sun was hotter than ever.

I followed the dirt road for about fifteen minutes as it narrowed into just a thin path. I was entranced with the idea that the Dark Swamp did exist after all. I noticed an abundance of wildlife: squirrels, rabbits, chipmunks and birds. As I walked on I thought that perhaps no one had traveled this path since 1923 when Lovecraft himself had come to Dark Swamp.

It was strange, though, that Lovecraft had never written

about the place, either in his journals or his letters. C. M. Eddy had written of the first unsuccessful trip, when he had accompanied Lovecraft, but aside from that the Dark Swamp was never mentioned.

I supposed it would remain a mystery, unless the swamp turned out to be not even worth writing about at all.

The path ended abruptly and the forest looked like it had not been trodden in years. I noticed the sudden absence of birds or other wildlife. The trees grew thicker and the ground became moist, dotted with small mushrooms and fungi. The sunlight became more faint; but the heat intensified as the forest thickened.

Finally, I found myself walking through thick mud. I continued on, thankful that I had worn my old sneakers, and stopped occasionally to adjust my flash unit and take a photograph.

The mud deepened with each step and the sunlight dimmed. I cursed myself for not bringing a flashlight, but I never expected the tales of the Dark Swamp to be so accurate—at least not as far as the darkness was concerned.

Suddenly all trace of light ended with a single step. Although I could not see into the blackness, my senses warned me about the swamp just ahead. There was an eerie stillness, and not even a mosquito disturbed the calm. The air stank of death and decay, as if some huge creature had been rotting away in the humidity for the last two thousand years.

So this was the Dark Swamp, I thought, still wishing I'd brought along a flashlight. At least I had a powerful flash unit on my camera. I'd take a couple of pictures to use with my article and I'd be in business. Excitedly I fumbled with the camera, adjusting the fluorescent dials in the darkness. I decided to take several pictures, just to make sure. The swamp was frightening enough and I had no desire to return if the pictures failed to come out.

As I lifted the camera I became aware of the overpowering odor; it was the same stench of death and decay magnified a

hundred times. Strangely enough, there was not even the slightest hint of a breeze to stir the air, and there was no wind to fan the disgusting smell towards me.

Ignoring the smell as best I could, I lifted the camera and snapped the shutter. The brilliant light of the flash illuminated the swamp for a fraction of a second.

I will never forget that instant. The image will remain welded into my brain for as long as I may live. I will remember each and every vivid detail, each shadow, each tiny reflection of light. I will relive the moment each night, in terrible dreams, and I will live each day in fear.

The swamp itself seemed black, even under the unnatural light. There were no trees, merely the empty blackness of the swamp. Yet somehow, though there was no shade, sunlight could not enter the place or pierce the darkness.

But it was more than this violation of physical laws that caused me to turn and flee from the Dark Swamp, that made me run the entire distance back through the woods and into my car, that made me speed away and not slow down until I had reached the familiar surroundings of Providence. Indeed, it was more than this. For in the swamp I saw a figure wading through the murky waters, wading towards the shore, its yellow eyes blazing with hatred and evil, and its fangs dripping with blood. What I saw in the terrible brackish waters was one of the Old Ones themselves, awakened from the deepest reaches of the swamp.

As I said, I fled and did not slow down until I reached Providence. I drove more slowly then, and my nerves had almost returned to normal when I reached my home in the suburbs. I began to doubt what I'd seen. I decided that it must have been the eerie setting coupled with a strange reflection of light that caused the apparition. I tried to calm myself, and almost succeeded. Then I remembered the camera. Surely the picture would prove that nothing existed in the Dark Swamp.

Relieved, I hurried to my darkroom and removed the film. Slowly, painstakingly, I developed the pictures, one by one,

calming myself with my work. Not until I had finished exposing the photographs of the dirt road, the forest, and the old woman did I reach the picture of the Dark Swamp. Tensely I waited for the image to appear on the paper. Nervously, I watched as it formed, the dark waters, the absence of any trees—and the figure of the Old One, bloated and toad-like as it walked from the swamp.

I screamed, alone in the darkroom, then opened the door and ran into the light.

It was almost an hour before I had the courage to return. Not until I had made three prints was I sure that the thing was real.

It's evening now. The darkness has descended much too quickly, and my hands tremble even as I write. The thing from the swamp needs darkness and Chepatchet is not so far from here. And I cannot help but remember the words of the old woman who sold vegetables by the side of the road. I remember what she said about the swamp and about the evil that lurks there: "These demons are just waiting to be let out, just waiting to escape and invade the world of men."

I shudder whenever I think about it. And I wonder if I am the one who set them free.

SAINT FRANCIS
OF THE DAMNED

I'm not sure which one of us spotted the injured pigeon first, but Mary swears it was me. I don't suppose it really matters because neither of us would have been able to leave the creature lying there in that cold puddle of water in the Burger King parking lot. Once we saw it, we were done for, and nothing would have been able to stop the intricate chain of events that followed, a chain of events that led up to horrors that I never could have imagined.

But then, on that October evening just before sunset, my life seemed as mundane and ordinary as it could possibly be.

I must confess, I almost didn't pick the bird up. I was sure it was dead. But Mary was just as sure it wasn't.

"Oh, Fran, it's hurt real bad," she said. "We can't just leave it there to die."

As if understanding her words the bird looked right at me and blinked. He was flattened out like he'd been hit by a truck and I didn't have much hope for him.

"Do you think we should move him" I asked.

"Well we can't just leave him there."

"I guess you're right," I said. "Maybe if we at least bring him over to the grass...."

So I reached down and gathered the bird in my hands, expecting half of his insides to drop out when I lifted him. But there was no blood and he accepted my help calmly, without attempting to peck or flee. I supposed that the poor creature was

probably in shock from whatever had happened to him.

I carried him over to a small traffic island at the front of the parking lot to set him down. But I noticed that the grass was teaming with red ants.

"I can't leave him here," I said to Mary, and pointed to the ground. "The ants will get him."

So it was decided. We brought him back to the car, wrapped him up in a beach blanket left over from the summer, and brought him home.

Both Mary and I knew that keeping an injured bird in a one-bedroom apartment with two predatory cats would never work. So Mary immediately began making phone calls: to local vets, animal shelters, pet stores—anyone who wouldn't hang up on her. An injured pigeon isn't the easiest thing to evoke sympathy for—I'm sure we'd have had an easier time with a robin or a cardinal—but after several referrals (a friend of a friend of a vet) Mary finally reached an old woman named Francis who told us to wrap the bird up and bring it to her right away.

The woman lived on the East Side of Providence somewhere off Benefit Street in the oldest section of town. We got lost twice trying to find the place and had to park in an alley, but we finally made it. I hadn't been to the East Side much, except for the bookstores on Thayer Street, and remember thinking that I'd traveled 200 years into the past.

If only I'd known then.

The house itself was mostly hidden behind an enormous hedge at the end of a dark cobblestone driveway. If it hadn't been for the full moon I doubt if I would have been able to make it; the only other light was the tiny glow of the doorbell.

I rang the bell and a light switched on, revealing an aging house in quite a state of disrepair. Most of the front porch had been transformed into a huge aviary for mourning doves. The birds flinched slightly when the light went on, and regarded me with interest.

Just as I pushed my head to the screen to see inside, a huge black and white cat jumped onto the ledge just in front of me,

nearly startling me to death. The cat glanced once at the birds through the cage, then looked back at me, as if to show that doves didn't excite him in the least. A small pathway led from the outside door and past the aviary to the inside door. I heard a slow shuffling coming closer from inside the house. Finally, the door opened and an old woman hobbled out.

The old lady was probably the least attractive specimen of humanity that I have ever seen. Although I later learned that she was only in her sixties, she appeared to be well over eighty. Her face was wrinkled like a metro-city roadmap, highlighted with several warts and moles. She had more hair on her chin than on her head, thin rat-grey hair, but long and stringy. She wore a dirty flannel bathrobe, even though it was only eight o'clock on a very warm evening. As she walked, she crouched forward and groaned with each step. A huge hump disfigured her back, making it impossible to stand up straight.

She stepped closer and peered at us through the screen door, scrutinizing us as if we were asking her to grant us a used car loan.

The woman was ugly, and borderline hideous. But her eyes were kind.

Mary and I must have passed whatever test the woman gave us because she opened the door, though just a crack.

"Let me see the bird."

Mary handed him over, and the woman took him, handling him gently but with polish and expertise. She obviously knew what she was doing as she flipped him over and examined his wing.

"It's a juvenile," she said, half to herself and half for our benefit. "The wing is broken...badly broken. No internal bleeding, though. The leg is broken too. I'd guess a cat or other animal got him."

"Can you fix him?" Mary asked.

"I'll have to set the wing," she said, still muttering to herself, even though she was answering my wife's question. "And splint the leg. But his heartbeat and lungs are strong. He's been in

shock but is coming out of it now."

Then she looked directly at us.

"He'll live," she pronounced.

Both Mary and I breathed a sigh of relief. This pigeon had become important to us.

"You know, not many people will handle pigeons," she said. "Most people consider them vermin. But they don't transmit disease. Even if they're sick, humans can't catch it."

She then continued with a long and detailed speech about the importance of pigeons in history, citing their ability to carry messages, and how they had been decisive in several battles. The woman sounded remarkably like a teacher—biology, I would have guessed.

I sort of drifted off during the woman's speech, but Mary began to warm up to her. The woman explained that she took in all kinds of stray and injured animals and nursed them back to health. But her health was deteriorating fast, making it more and more difficult for her to keep up with even the routine chores. Mary felt sorry for the woman and gave her some money to help pay for the upkeep of the bird, and she suggested to her that we might volunteer to help her out.

It was with a profound sense of relief that we left the woman's house. I truly didn't expect to ever see her again, despite Mary's promises to help her out. I agreed that we should volunteer some of our time, but the challenges and demands of everyday life somehow have a way of getting in the way of the best intentions and I suspected that this case would be no different. That's why it came as a surprise when the old lady called two days later to report that the pigeon was doing fine and to ask if I could drop by and give her a hand. Mary was working late and I had nothing better to do, and my guilt was triggered by the woman's kindness, so I agreed to come over for a couple of hours.

It was just after eight p.m. when I arrived—this time I only got lost once. It had rained earlier in the day and I had to wade through a couple of good-sized puddles to get to the front door. I was annoyed because she didn't put the front light on, even

though she knew I was coming. I found out when she greeted me and told me that the bulb had burned out and she couldn't reach the socket to change it, so that was my first task.

After I changed the light bulb the old woman suggested that I accompany her on the evening feeding and check-up, so I'd know the routine. I agreed.

The place was much larger inside than what it appeared from outside, and it left me with the impression of walking through a giant maze. The place was really more of a zoo than a home, since she had cages everywhere in every available space. She had several walk-in aviaries for pigeons, doves, seagulls and crows and smaller cages for robins, sparrows, blue jays, and other assorted birds, some kinds of which I had never seen before. She had cages full of mice in the kitchen and cages full of finches in her bedroom. The living room contained cats and dogs in small kennels. Dozens of other cats and dogs roamed the house freely, walking wounded with bandages on their paws, heads, and tails.

"Every animal has its own special diet," she assured me, as she pointed out the various types of food.

The basement had a collection of more exotic animals, ferrets, snakes, lizards, a raccoon, two opossums, a fox and even a skunk.

"He won't spray," she said. "I've had him since he was a baby."

All of the animals seemed content and well-cared for, and I complimented the woman for her efforts.

"You're like Saint Francis," I said. "Taking care of all the sick and injured animals."

"You're a Saint Francis, too," she said, smiling for the first time, and only then was I struck by the coincidence of us both having the same first name.

Just as we were about to leave, a horrible scream sounded from the far end of the basement. I rushed over to see, only to find a padlocked door with a do not enter sign on it.

"Oh, no, don't go in there!" the old lady said, trembling

violently.

Another scream almost rattled the very walls.

"What is that?" I said.

"Please...don't go in there," she said.

"Someone—or something—is hurt in there! It sounds like you've got a person locked up in there!"

All I could picture was someone chained up in the basement and being tortured—like something out of a V.C. Andrews book. I looked back at the old lady and I knew she was insane.

"Open the door!" I commanded.

"You can't go in there!"

I grabbed a crowbar in the tool area and began working on the lock. The screaming began again. Just as I popped the lock open, I looked up in time to see the old woman about to hit me with a hammer.

I ducked, but she managed to clip me on the ear. It hurt like hell but wasn't serious. I backed away as she advanced on me with the weapon.

"Listen, lady," I said. "I don't want any trouble...."

Suddenly she didn't look as old or as feeble, and I imagined myself about to join her other captive in the back room of the basement. I couldn't let that happen. I'd take the old witch out first.

I ducked my head down and charged forward, sidestepping at the last moment as she swung the hammer down at me. She caught my elbow as I went by, but I was so pumped up I didn't even feel the pain until later. I reacted strictly by instinct as I put every ounce of my strength into an uppercut to her lower jaw. Dazed, she sprawled backwards, dropping the hammer and falling back against the wall.

I'd temporarily forgotten about the screaming from behind the door. But another shriek reminded me of it. The old lady was between me and the door, but before I could try to get past her, the padlock popped free where I'd broken it and the door opened outward.

The old lady was just coming to when she realized the door

was open.

"No!" she screamed. "Not me! Not me!"

It happened so fast I wasn't even sure what I saw at the time. I know there was a huge, leathery wing, like that of a bat, only a vertical wing instead of the horizontal type that bats have. And there was a claw—I did see the claw very clearly. It had long, sharp talons and human-like fingers—kind of like a gorilla's hand only with an eagle's claws. The old woman's flesh tore where the thing grabbed her and she screamed.

The creature from inside the locked room pulled her back inside. She tried to wrap her leg around the door before it closed, and that bought her just about ten seconds. It wasn't very long but it was long enough.

In those ten seconds I saw her anguish and her pain. And I heard her final words.

"Someone needs to take care of them too," she said, looking directly into my eyes. "The demons and the monsters. They get hurt too. And now it falls to you, Saint Francis. Saint Francis of the Damned. Remember, they each have a special diet."

And then the gargoyle thing pulled hard and she was gone. I rushed to close and lock the door behind them. Then I collapsed by the door and listened to the terrible sounds of the creature feeding.

So now it falls to me, the new Saint Francis of the Damned. Because the old lady was right. Someone has to take care of them. And even if I leave here, I know they will seek me out.

I don't know how I will tell Mary, or if I'll even tell her at all. I suppose I'll have to. She'll come looking and the police will get involved. And if I don't show her what lives in the cages in the very back room, she may find out for herself and that would not be good.

Mary is very kind and loves animals, so it will be a good life. I just wish there was a way to keep her from knowing about the creatures in the back room—the ones with the special diet.

THE MAN WHO
COLLECTED BEAUTY

The man with the jet-black suit strolled by the gallery every day at two o'clock sharp. Christie had actually begun to look for him now, and to expect him.

He was a creepy old man, she thought, as she sat on the bar stool behind the counter and watched the traffic on Wickenden Street and waited for him to come by. Yes, creepy and kind of scary, but fascinating too, in a perverse sort of way. At first she had dreaded his walks and had been worried that he might actually step inside the gallery. But after three full weeks of the daily ritual, she now looked forward to the break in her dull routine. And some small part of her actually wished he *would* come in.

She recalled seeing him for the first time on her first day on the job. She'd been busy unwrapping a UPS shipment of pottery and was bending down behind the counter to take a piece from the box. When she straightened up she had seen him—a wild, turbulent-looking face watching her through the glass window.

She'd shrieked in terror, and, startled by the sudden apparition, almost dropped the $500 ceramic vase she'd been unpacking. By the time she'd regained control of the vase and placed it on the counter, he was gone.

The next day he had come back and this time, although she was still frightened, she was no longer startled. She'd had a better chance to examine him as he stopped and looked in the window for about half a minute, and then resumed his stroll.

His hair was feathery white, like a swan, and his blue eyes stared out of bony sockets and seemed to look right through her. He always wore the same suit—black, like that of a funeral director, with a white shirt and thin black tie. Like one of the Blues Brothers, she thought, only without the hat and shades. Every day he would stop for a moment, peer at whatever was in the window, look briefly at her, and then move on. On slow days where there were no customers and no deliveries to unpack, it was her only distraction for the entire day.

And today was one of those slow days.

Christie still wasn't sure why she'd taken the job at the gallery. She didn't particularly like art and she really didn't like dealing with the public—especially some of the snotty professors from Brown and RISD who looked down their nose at her. Little did they know that she had come from more money than they could ever dream of, and if her stupid husband hadn't gambled it all away she might very well be one of the big spenders at the gallery.

Actually, it would be her interior designer who would be doing all of the spending, she thought. She wouldn't waste her time shopping for art—not when she could be at the new Providence Place Mall buying expensive clothes. That would suit the ex-Miss South Carolina just fine. She stole a look in the mirror beside the cash register and smiled her patented beauty-pageant smile, big and bright and as phony as ten-carat rhinestone. Her long, black hair was as shiny as ever, and her black eyes calculating, as always. Yes, she looked better than ever, she thought. If only she hadn't married that loser.…

Just then the two-o'clock chime went off from the $200 original Deidre Martin clock on the wall. She looked towards the street and frowned. The old man was late today.

She stood up, stretched, and tried to interest herself in the traffic outside as the minutes ticked by. It wasn't like him to be late, she thought. Maybe he was sick or had an accident. Or maybe he'd just been distracted by another pretty girl in another shop window. A bit of jealousy rushed to Christie's face at the

thought. There couldn't possibly be anyone prettier than her, not in this shabby street in this shabby town.

Anxious, she walked over to the door so she could look down the street. Maybe he was just late after all.

As she put her head out the doorway to look, he appeared, so suddenly and silently that it might have been by magic. A gasp rushed from her throat as she recoiled from his presence and ducked back inside. He stopped and looked at her with interest, capturing her eyes with his own, deep and blue and piercing. His eyes were as calculating as her own and somehow, she thought, he didn't look old anymore.

"Excuse me," he said in a smooth, even voice, a voice like melted butter. "I didn't mean to startle you."

"Oh...I'm...no you didn't startle me...I was just...."

The man smiled. It wasn't the first time he'd caught her by surprise and he knew it.

"I...ah...I see you walk by every day at this time," Christie said, trying to change the subject. "You always look in the window."

"Yes," he replied. "You have such beautiful things here. I am a collector."

"Oh, I see," she said. "A collector. What, exactly, do you collect?"

The man looked at her for a long moment, examining her as if she were a fine porcelain bowl.

"I collect beauty."

Christie frowned. The man had a touch of an accent, which she couldn't place.

"Oh, you collect beautiful things?"

"No," he corrected. "I collect beauty."

Christie looked at him for a moment and didn't know what to say. She took a step back into the store, then, remembering where she was, turned back towards him.

"Then perhaps I could show you some of the beauty that we have in the gallery," she said, flashing her best salesperson smile.

"You already have," he said softly. "Every day when I look in your window."

But he followed her inside, nonetheless.

"We've just received some new work by Karl Petersen," she said, showing him the display she'd finished setting up that morning. "He does some very fine work."

The man stepped over to the display and admired the pottery, touching one bowl gently, as one might touch a butterfly's wings.

"It is very beautiful," he said.

Christie took a moment to examine the man more closely as he admired the work. His suit was definitely high quality, tailored to fit just right. And he wore an expensive pair of Italian leather shoes. Christie knew that you judged a man by his shoes and a woman by her purse—both were sure indicators of a person's wealth. Judging from his shoes this man could easily afford anything in the gallery.

"We also have some new paintings from Elizabeth Corbeil," Christie said, reciting her sales pitch perfectly. "Her work has recently gone on exhibit at the Boston Museum of Fine Arts."

The man looked to where she pointed and studied the art for a moment. It was a modern piece, colorful and abstract.

"Hmmm," he said. "It is interesting. But I'm afraid I'm more of a conservative. I prefer the more classical beauty."

He looked directly into Christie's eyes as he spoke, and if the man hadn't been so refined she would have thought that he was hitting on her. But his look was more clinical than sensual, as if he were an art critic and she was the masterpiece. Something about the look made Christie shiver, even though it was a warm October day.

Then you might wish to see the work of Jean-Claude Vienne," she said. "His work is very traditional."

"I'm afraid my tastes lean towards the very exquisite," the man said. "The work here is very beautiful, but I'm afraid that I've grown very selective with age. I no longer buy everything I see."

Christie felt for a moment that she was being insulted. But

the man couldn't possibly know her passion for buying new things just for the sake of buying new things.

"One eventually gets to the point where there just isn't enough room to collect everything one sees," he continued.

Christie smiled. "Yes, a man such as yourself must be very discriminating."

The man nodded.

"I have seen one object of beauty that I would desire," he said, looking at her.

Christie forced back a blush and refused to drop her eyes. Now, refined or not, she was convinced that he *was* hitting on her after all. But that was to be expected. All men did, sooner or later. They just couldn't help themselves and by now she was accustomed to it.

"You are a very beautiful woman," he continued, still looking into her eyes, as if he could hypnotize her with his wealth.

"I am afraid that I am not for sale, Sir," Christie said, firmly but very diplomatically, with a sweet voice that could cut a man to the quick and still leave him smiling.

"No, you mistake me," the man said. "I do not wish to buy you."

"Then what do you wish?"

"I wish to buy your beauty."

Christie broke out in a sudden laugh.

"You want to buy my beauty? That's the most ridiculous thing I've ever heard. I couldn't sell you that, even if I wanted to."

"Name your price," the man said, very softly, very seriously.

Christie laughed again and shook her head.

"You're joking, right? I mean, even if I wanted to sell my beauty, how could I? It's not just the kind of thing you can peel off and give away...."

The man pulled a small black camera from his inside jacket pocket and placed it on the counter. Christie looked at it for a moment.

"Oh...you want to take my picture? That's all?"

"I want to buy your beauty," the man insisted, and then took out his wallet.

Slowly and very carefully, he pulled out twenty one-hundred-dollar bills and placed them, one at a time, beside the camera.

"Will this suffice?"

Christie looked down at the money and then back at the man. Two thousand dollars for letting this old geezer take her picture, she thought. This guy must be crazy. Definitely senile. But two thousand dollars. Wouldn't that buy a few new things at the mall.

"Just my picture, right? I don't have to take off my clothes or do anything kinky?"

"I just want your beauty," the man replied.

Christie looked at him again, thought of the new stores opening up at the mall, and then decided.

"Ok. What do you want me to do. As long as I don't have to take my clothes off."

"That won't be necessary," the man said. "Just stand by the window and I'll do the rest."

She went behind the counter and looked in the mirror. Not bad, she thought, but for $2,000 she figured she'd better give this old man his money's worth. She pulled her makeup bag from her purse and touched up a bit, fluffed her hair and smiled.

"Ok, I'm ready."

The man picked up the camera and nodded as she walked over to the window and assumed her familiar beauty pageant pose. This was surely the easiest money she'd ever earned, and tax free even.

"Click away," she said.

The man raised the camera and peered through the view-finder while Christie held her smile, just like they'd taught her in charm school. She waited patiently while the man did whatever it was that you do with a camera when taking a picture. Then she heard the telltale click of the shutter.

There was no flash, but for a moment everything around her seemed a bright shade of red. Then it was gone and the man

lowered the camera.

"You can take a couple more if you'd like," she said, striking another beauty queen pose.

"That won't be necessary," he said. "I have what I want."

He smiled at her, but his smile now seemed strange and he no longer met her eyes. Then he hurried from the gallery, cradling the camera as if it had somehow become a priceless treasure.

Christie shook her head in confusion.

"That was one weird old man," she said out loud as she made her way back behind the counter. "Two thousand dollars for one lousy picture."

She picked up the money and counted it carefully. It was all there. And it would buy her some wonderful new outfits, the kind that she had been used to wearing when she had money. But it also felt a bit strange, as if a chapter in her life had ended. She was certain that the old man would no longer come around at two o'clock each day. She would never see him again. And she was sorry for that. But, in a way that she couldn't quite understand, she was also grateful, because now she had no desire to ever see him again. What she'd thought had been an interesting and intriguing old man had turned out to be quite ordinary after all, just another old man who wanted her, in his own strange way.

But she had a nagging feeling that something was not right. He had wanted to buy her beauty.

With sudden shock and insight she turned to look in the mirror thinking, even as she did so, that it couldn't be real, that she had just become paranoid and foolish, like an old lady believing in the most ridiculous superstition. Yet something also told her that it *was* real, and she knew it was real before she even looked, and that knowledge was what kept her from screaming.

A strange face stared back at her from the mirror. It was a plain face, pock-marked and scarred, with drab, mousy-brown hair and dull eyes that had lost all trace of beauty. She stared, open-mouthed at her reflection, hoping that it was some sort of perverted practical joke that he'd played with a fake mirror but

knowing all the time that it was no joke, that it was real and that it was true. It wasn't an ugly face, really, she thought. Just plain. Ordinary. Average. The kind of face that would never stand out in a crowd.

That's when Christie did scream. When she realized that now she was no better or worse than anyone else.

And the man who collected beauty heard her scream and smiled.

LADY OF THE NIGHT

Stan waited behind the spruce trees outside the door, seething in anger as he shivered in the cold. It was Beth all right, he thought for the tenth time in as many minutes. Her footprints clearly led up the snow-covered walk to the front door, where she'd lost a single red high-heeled shoe just before she went inside.

Beth and his best friend John had been making eyes at one another all afternoon at his cousin's wedding. Then, when he'd woken up at four o'clock in the morning, he'd found his bed empty and the front door wide open.

It wasn't the first time his wife had disappeared in the night. But this time it would be the last.

He pulled the sleek, deadly bowie knife from its sheath and looked at it lovingly. It was a parting gift from his father, who'd used it to slit his own wrists when Stan was just sixteen. Good riddance to the bastard, he thought, remembering the beatings and abuse.

Tonight, he'd put his dear old dad's gift to good use.

While he knew he'd have to move quietly, he also realized he'd need to act before the first light of dawn. Beth had always returned home at dawn. Several times he'd pretended to be asleep. This time he'd know for sure.

He crept out from behind the spruce trees and smudged out his wife's footprints as he made his way to the door. Luck was with him: she'd left this door open as well, saving him the trouble of picking the lock, or breaking a window, which might

have alerted them.

He grinned as he nudged the door open. He'd show them. He'd show them both. He might not be the smartest man alive, but no one played him for the fool.

With the deliberate care of a stalking cat, he entered the living room. Only the sound of his best friend's grandfather clock broke the silence. Good, he thought. They were probably both sleeping. And they'd wake up dead, he thought, liking the way the expression sounded in his mind. He stifled the urge to say it aloud—wake up dead.

John would go first, he decided as he snuck towards the bedroom. After all, Beth was a beautiful woman and he really couldn't blame his friend for wanting her. It was Beth's fault. You just couldn't trust a woman. So he'd kill John quickly, in his sleep. Then he'd make his wife pay the price.

He reached the bedroom and eased open the door. Already the first light of dawn had filtered through the window, highlighting a shadowy form on the bed. The lovers intertwined? Or maybe she'd already escaped through the back door.

He moved forward to the bed and, even as he recognized John's naked form, he knew something was wrong. The sickening, almost metallic small of blood reached his nostrils as he saw the open wound where his friend's insides had been ripped out.

"Oh my God," he whispered.

His stomach flipped, but before he could retch he heard a low, throaty growl from the center of the room, and he focused on a pair of demon-like yellow eyes staring at him from the darkness.

He barely had time to brace himself as the eyes suddenly leaped forward, and a drooling jaw full of hungry teeth lunged towards him. His reflexes reacted and he ducked to the side and swiped forward with his knife, all in one motion. The quick but powerful cut connected with bone, and the creature yelped like a kicked dog. It landed in a heap, flashed him a parting look of hatred, and then scuttled from the room and out the door.

Stan fell back onto the bed, where he found himself sitting on something. Vaguely wondering what had happened to Beth, he reached down and picked up a severed paw. He'd cut it off at the ankle.

The shade had been left open, and the sun rose quickly now, bathing the wolfish limb in a new light. It was changing already, and, with sudden horror, Stan knew why his wife preferred the night.

The fingers were almost fully human now, and on the third digit he recognized a familiar object. It was the gold wedding band he'd placed on Beth's finger almost three years ago.

Beth never had liked silver, he thought.

THOSE WHO FAVOR FIRE

Some say the world will end in fire,
Some say ice.
From what I've tasted of desire
I hold with those who favor fire.
　　　　　　　　—Robert Frost

Brady Edwards was one of those who favored fire. The flames drew him in with their brilliant reds and oranges, their dazzling yellows, and especially the vivid blues and purples, where the heat was most intense. He loved fires. He loved to watch them. He loved to paint them. He loved having painted them. Yet he'd grown to hate, to fear the paintings. And the fires. Tonight would be his last.

Brady sat down on his cot and looked around his small studio workplace and residence in AS220 where, after almost two years on the waiting list, his number had finally come up and he'd been assigned a place to live and to paint. He looked at the collection of paintings that lined the wall—fifteen of them in all, one of them for each of the Providence WaterFires he had attended and painted, beginning at the end of May. It was October now, two days before Halloween, and this would be his last.

He did not want to go. But he needed to. The fires drew him like a moth to the flames, and like the moth, he knew the flames would end in his own destruction. He looked at the painting he had created and knew tonight would be his undoing. But he

simply could not stop himself.

It had taken him months to come to grips with what was happening to him and he still wasn't sure if he'd suddenly become extremely lucid, or if he'd just gone insane. He wondered if you could go insane, like that—all of a sudden lose your mind. He wasn't sure. But when he looked back on it he realized it hadn't been so sudden after all, not really. It had happened gradually, beginning with the first WaterFire at the end of May. Only by looking back at all of the paintings in sequence was he really able to understand what was happening.

Before returning to Providence in May, he'd spent two years painting sunsets on Mallory Square in Key West after dropping out of art school in the middle of his freshman year when his Painting I professor had pronounced him merely "an illustrator—and not a very good one at that." Sunsets were fires in their own right, he now realized, with their dazzling mix of reds, yellows, and oranges. He had left behind his demons and catered to tourists, leaving nothing behind except an application form for residency at AS220, which he'd forgotten about once he'd left Providence.

He'd been full of passion and ambition when he'd entered art school. He particularly loved fantasy art, dragons, demons, wizards, and heroes with swords. Inspired by the fiction of Tolkien and Robert E. Howard, he'd painted a particularly realistic demonic creature, flaming in reds and oranges and yellows, and garnished with a coppery green face emerging from the flames. He'd always been attracted by fire. He supposed it was the superbly elemental force that could never quite be tamed.

When his turn had come up, he'd proudly displayed his work on the easel at the front of the class. The colors leaped off the canvas, creating an almost photographic image of something that never was, and could not ever be.

The professor had walked slowly up to the painting, stroking his beard thoughtfully as he studied the work. Brady felt his heart fluttering in his chest. This was the first time anyone but his family had seen his paintings, and he was anxious for some

validation of his work. He knew he had talent—everyone he knew told him so—but this was different.

The professor slowly turned around and faced the class of twenty-five freshmen with that smug look of arrogance that only those who teach but do not do can sometimes have, and then he looked directly at Brady. The look said it all. And then with a single, smooth cut to the neck he lowered his axe in a clean, neat execution that didn't even bleed until hours later when Brady was walking home along the Providence River canal with his painting tucked securely under his arm. Then, and only then, did the numbness leave and the sting begin. It hurt like hell.

He stopped beside the river and sat on one of the benches overlooking the water. First he wept with the deep, quaking sorrow of dashed dreams. Then anger set in, with its fraternal twin, frustration. In a fit of rage, Brady placed his painting on the bench, set it on fire with a disposable Bic lighter, and then threw the flaming mess into the river. He watched as it burned like a funeral pyre and then sank slowly out of sight.

Brady had walked away from the river, walked away from art school, and walked away from Providence, vowing to never come back. He never went back to the school, not even to retrieve his cache of paints and brushes from the studio classroom where he'd been assigned space. He'd never seen nor heard from the professor again, though not a week went by without him wishing a horrible curse upon him and everything he held dear.

Brady never painted demons again, or wizards or dragons either. He'd hitchhiked on Route 1 until he could go no further, to what seemed like the ends of the earth—or at least the end of America—and found himself in Key West. He found he had a knack for painting sunsets, at least the tourists thought so, and he was able to make a living painting his own versions of fire. Maybe the professor had been right. He was just an illustrator—and not a very good one at that. But the tourists bought his work faster than he could paint it, and he liked painting solar fire.

He'd returned to Providence in May when he'd received a forwarded letter saying that he was next on the list for a resi-

dential place at AS220. If it had come at any other time he would have turned it down. But the thought of facing another scorching South Florida summer followed by another hurricane season was just too much to bear. Ironically, it turned out to be one of the hottest summers in Rhode Island history, but he'd had no way of knowing that when he accepted the offer to return.

And somehow, on the last Saturday night in May, he'd found himself sitting on that same bench by the River, looking out into the water, carrying everything he owned: a canvas backpack with a change of clothes, a set of latex paints heavy in reds, yellows, and oranges with just a hint of blue, green, and purple, a single blank canvas, a portable easel, and just over $6,000 in cash that he'd earned by painting one fifty-dollar sunset at a time.

He found himself sitting on that beach staring into the water to the very place where he'd exorcised his demon-painting over two years ago. Once again, he was looking at fire. The WaterFire.

He'd known about the famous Providence WaterFires, of course—how could he not have? They had become an institution in the city, lighting up the river and the canal with dozens of bonfires in the water. But he'd never attended one. And he'd never intended to come to this one on his first night back, either. He'd simply been drawn to that place of his earlier misery, much as a salmon returns to the same place to spawn. Without knowing why, he'd simply found himself there by the canal looking at the water. And then, as the sun went down, as if by magic, there had been fire.

Without thought or effort, he'd pulled out his blank canvas and had painted furiously, capturing it all in a flurry of reds, oranges, yellows, blues, purples, and a little green. He'd captured it all, the eerie, hauntingly beautiful music, the snapping, crackling of the sparks from the fire, the cedar forest scent of the smoke, so exhilarating and new. He'd captured it all in brilliant flowing colors so bold against a background of black, with shadowy figures in boats watching the display.

When he returned home to his studio, he realized it was the most amazing piece of work he had ever done. He'd returned to each WaterFire throughout the summer and into the fall. Each time, he'd gone to the same bench, arrived early to stake out a spot, and had painted until his fingers were numb.

Now, on the last Saturday night of October, just two days before Halloween, he looked over his collection of WaterFire paintings, fifteen of them. They hung on an otherwise blank wall, a fearful procession of flames that became more and more menacing with each try. As he looked at each of them, he could see his own demon emerging from the flames. Each night it had grown larger and more distinct. It had become more angry—and more bold.

He examined the first one, done so unwittingly on the Memorial Day weekend. At first glance it looked like nothing more than flames, the essence of the art that was WaterFire, a brilliant pyre of flames rising from the ink, with a mirrored, rippled reflection. It was mostly the hot colors, reds, yellows, orange, with some blue and purple. But at the center was a twinge of green.

Copper, he'd thought at the time. Copper burns green. There must have been some copper on the logs, or in an accelerant.

He hadn't noticed the face in the flames until later, after he'd completed two more, on the 5th of June to be exact. The green seemed to have eyes that looked out at him.

The face was far more pronounced in the second painting. But he still didn't notice it until the third, where the two eyes were quite distinct, as was the beginning of a mouth, framed in blue and violet. By the fourth paining, the reds and oranges raged forth like appendages reaching out and up into the night air.

By the ninth painting the face was distinct, and by the twelfth, it was exact, with a unique expression and an unmistakable demonic face. He'd questioned his own perception, and had shown it to Bert, the artistic director and an accomplished artist himself.

Bert immediately pointed out the demonic qualities without being asked, and pronounced the painting beautiful, frightening, and intensely realistic.

"Very symbolic," Bert had said. "You've captured the demon within all of us."

Bert had offered to hang the paintings in the downstairs gallery in time for the last WaterFire, but Brady had refused.

"They're not complete," he'd said by way of an excuse. "The WaterFire season's not over."

Bert had reluctantly agreed. "After the October fires, then. Then we'll have a complete set."

By the fourteenth painting, Brady had almost convinced himself that the paintings really were symbolic, and nothing more. But something wasn't quite right and he knew it. The demon was more than symbolic, he feared. It was real. Furthermore, it was his demon and his alone.

Two weeks ago, during the last WaterFire, he'd brought along a camera he'd borrowed from one of the other residents, and he'd taken some pictures of the fires, then had gone ahead and completed his painting. Later, after he'd processed the pictures, the film confirmed what he feared the most. The demon in the flames was real. Worse, it was growing larger, growing stronger, growing nearer…and it was coming for him.

He looked at the new painting now, number 15, a larger, expanded image of the 8½" x 11" photo enlargement he'd made. Both the painting and the photo showed the same thing. The green dominated the center of the flames now. Its features were distinct. Serpent-like malicious eyes with a coppery tint. A leering, scornful mouth, like that of his art professor, only with vicious, drooling fangs, tipped with drops of blood. Flared, gaping nostrils, snorting hate. And now, on the fringes of the flame, long, needle-like crimson claws reaching out for him.

It was his demon, his dragon that he had set on fire and thrown into the river so long ago. It was his demon, which he had tried so hard to burn, to bury, to drown. It was coming back and it was angry.

Brady didn't think it could be put down. It had come back in the fire. It showed itself in his painting, and in the photographs; it was plain for anyone to see.

Tonight, he would face that demon. He would accept it as his own and would paint it as faithfully and accurately as if it were a Key West sunset. It would be terrifying, and there would be those who would prefer the innocuous, harmless sunsets. But he needed to face this demon; he would face it, and by painting it, he would recapture it and tame it once and forever.

After that, who knew what he would paint? He would go wherever his demon led him.

But he knew the demon would try to destroy him first. It was coming for him. But he would be ready. Carefully, he gathered his paints, his canvas, his portable easel. He would need more green and blue tonight.

He looked around his studio one last time. He'd need to leave now if he wanted to get his usual spot before the crowds arrived. He wondered if he could really cage and chain this demon to the canvas. It didn't really matter. He had no choice. The flames called to him, as if he were a moth, pulling him closer. Even if he wanted to, he couldn't ignore the call.

For he was one of those who favored fire.

NIGHTMARE

For the third night in a row the familiar black horse appeared outside and stood waiting and looking at him from the nursing home parking lot. Despite the chill October air, John supported himself with his cane and slid the large window open. The nurses would have a fit when they found out and would return him to his room, but he figured he had a few minutes until they tracked him down in the day room.

I've obviously lost my mind, he thought. There aren't any horses on the East Side of Providence, no way, no how, not for a hundred years, he guessed. But the horse flared its nostrils audibly, taking in his scent, and then nickered a greeting as if they were old friends. If this were a hallucination, it was sure realistic—even the pleasant and familiar smell of the horse was unmistakable.

He hadn't been around horses in, what, ten years? Not since he'd moved back into the city, a mistake he had regretted ever since. But the new job was in the city and impossible to turn down; it demanded so much time that, even if it weren't for the hour-long commute, he wouldn't have been able to spend time with the horses anyway. Besides, his wife Ann had hated the country lifestyle and his horse business, which was, in all honesty, devouring his savings faster than an overweight teen at an all-you-can-eat buffet. So he'd sold the barn and the horses, came out of early retirement, and taken the position at the bank where his first assignment was to cut costs and eliminate jobs.

It had hurt, all right. But selling the black mare, the one he'd

named Nightmare, had hurt the worst. She was more a friend than a horse, and the only one who really loved him. And, yes, his years working with horses had convinced him that horses were truly capable of giving and receiving love—but they did not give that gift of love easily or to just anyone.

He'd bought Nightmare for Ann in the hope that she'd take an interest in his hobby, but she would rather buy fancy clothes and go to social functions than hang around with a horse. She might ride the mare twice a year, if John got her cleaned and ready and saddled. Ann would then climb on and sit up there on the saddle like a monkey as the horse walked her around. She thought that was riding.

But Nightmare had different ideas, and the horse had bonded with John, the man who took care of her and did most of the riding. Before long, the horse wouldn't even allow Ann to get near her, let alone ride.

He'd had her for two years, the best two years of his life, until he sold her to what he prayed was a good family, but when he tried to check on her later, they had disappeared and he feared the worst.

Now he looked out the window at this horse and knew that it was Nightmare. He'd recognize those soft, brown eyes anywhere, and the distinctive white crescent on her forehead. She even wore her old saddle, black with orange trim. It was perfect for Halloween, he thought. She nickered again, calling to him like she used to whenever he'd entered the stables.

"You are a foolish old man," he said out loud. "You're having delusions."

Taking the bank job had been a mistake, despite the obscene amount of money they paid him. He'd suffered his first heart attack at 60, just five years after selling his farm, and now this stroke had put him in a nursing home, and if Ann and his kids had their way, he'd never get out. Obviously, it must have messed up his brain, like they said, because here he was seeing horses in the parking lot every night.

"Nightmare," he whispered. "Where's my horse?"

It was the greeting he always used with her, and she used to respond to by walking over to him. Sure enough, she recognized it; the horse lowered her head and walked to the window and she pressed her nose to the screen. He reached out and touched her through the thin screen. Her warm breath warmed his hand.

"Well, if you are a delusion, you're sure better than anything I've had lately," he said.

The horse pushed forward, shoving her face through the window screen and into the room. She pushed the screen aside, ripping it like paper. John used his cane to peel back the debris.

"Nightmare," he said. "You wanna ride?"

The horse nickered. John grinned, grabbed the horse's neck, and pulled himself through the window. Somehow, his legs, his arms, everything worked perfectly and he was in the saddle.

"This is the best dream I've ever had," he said. "A Nightmare."

He leaned forward and wrapped his arms around the horse's neck, hugging her. Burying his cheek in her soft mane, he closed his eyes and drank in the moment. Then he sat tall in the saddle and patted her neck.

"Ok. Let's ride!"

Nightmare immediately backed up and turned around, facing the street. She had always been an active horse, and it seemed that she still wanted to go. She didn't seem to be a day older than when he'd sold her. And now that he was in the saddle, John didn't feel any older either. His legs were strong in the stirrups—he didn't need that stupid cane now. He felt ten years younger; come to think of it, maybe twenty.

He gave Nightmare the old cue and she was off, trotting down the parking lot and onto the sidewalk. She turned west, headed for Thayer Street, and he just let her go. The horse, apparently, had a plan and he wasn't about to interfere. He had always been the leader and in control of the horse. But he knew this ride was different. Nightmare knew where she was going.

It was well after midnight and the streets were deserted. The jack-o-lanterns and Halloween decorations had all been turned off in the yards and front stairs, and only the occasional car

went by and didn't seem to notice an old man riding a black horse. They blended very well into the night.

The traffic lights were blinking and the only noise was the rhythmic clopping of Nightmare's hooves on the sidewalk. To John, it was music.

As they approached Thayer Street, John expected to find some late night Halloween party goers, but Nightmare had something else planned. She made a sharp turn down a side street that John wasn't familiar with. There were no street lights—only the glow of the yellow half-moon in the sky. And the road, strangely enough, narrowed and turned into a dirt path. They were surrounded by trees, oak trees that hadn't shed their leaves yet. And the chill night air suddenly wasn't so chill anymore.

John felt the wind rush past him as Nightmare broke into a smooth canter in what appeared to be a large field. It was difficult to see in the dim light; the horse's night vision was much better than his, and her hooves pounded evenly on the ground. John leaned forward and patted the horse's neck. Cantering had always been the most fun for both of them. And for just a few moments, John was back on his farm, young and healthy and riding Nightmare across a clover field in the moonlight. It didn't get any better than this.

For an instant his thoughts drifted back to the nursing home. He'd obviously fallen asleep, probably in the day room, and the nurse would show up any minute and wake him up. Then, realizing how painful that waking up moment would be, he drove it from his mind.

Nightmare slowed to a walk and John realized that it was getting light. The sun was rising quickly and as he looked around he knew the dream had taken him far from the city. The pastures around him went for miles, flat grasslands without end. And ahead of him, another black horse lay in the field. Nightmare walked up to this horse and stopped. John looked down and realized that this horse was a mirror of the one he was riding. This was Nightmare too, only old, weak, and put out to pasture. She lifted her head weakly and nickered at him

in recognition. Then she lay back down and was still.

He looked at the prone horse for a long moment.

"So this is why you came to me," he said. "You're dying too."

The horse he was riding seemed more real than the one on the ground. This horse was, somehow, alive. He patted her gently on the neck. This was her way of coming to him for a ride so they could be together again, even if it was only in their dreams. She let out a long, loud whinny, reared slightly, and then turned her head around to look back at him. She wanted to run through the meadows. And she wanted him to come with her. He knew what she was asking—he could stay here or go back to the nursing home.

He didn't want this dream to end.

"Come on, girl," he said. "Let's run!"

Nightmare whinnied again and the man and his horse, both young and healthy, galloped off into the pasture. They rode off into the world where dreams come true and they never came back.

* * * * * * *

The nurse found John on the floor in the day room at first light, but it was too late. He'd suffered another stroke, a fatal one this time. They never could understand the broken window screen and the horse hoof prints just outside, or the huge smile on John's face. The charge nurse just shrugged.

"Must have been trick or treaters," she said as they took the body to the morgue. She knew there were no horses on the East Side.

ACKNOWLEDGMENTS

Some of these stories were previously published as follows, and are reprinted by permission of the author:

"The Date from Hell" was originally published in *East Side Monthly*, ed. by Barry Fain, October 2009. Copyright © 2009, 2013 by James Arthur Anderson.

"The Belfry" was originally published in *Weird Tales #4*, edited by Lin Carter, Zebra Books, 1983. Copyright © 1983, 2013 by James Arthur Anderson.

"My Canine Cutie" was originally published in *East Side Monthly*, ed. by Barry Fain, October 2012. Copyright © 2012, 2013 by James Arthur Anderson.

"The One That Got Away" was originally published in *East Side Monthly*, ed. by Barry Fain, October 1989. Copyright © 1989, 2013 by James Arthur Anderson.

"Manuscript Found in a Rare Book Store" was originally published in *East Side Monthly*, ed. by Barry Fain, October 2011. Copyright © 2011, 2013 by James Arthur Anderson.

"The Hatchling" was originally published in *East Side Monthly*, ed. by Barry Fain, October 1991. Copyright © 1991, 2013 by James Arthur Anderson.

"Dark Swamp" was originally published in *Eldritch Tales #9*, April 1983, ed. by Crispin Burnham, and reprinted in *The Tsathoggua Cycle*, ed. by Robert M. Price, Chaosium Books, 2005. Copyright © 1983, 2005, 2013 by James Arthur Anderson.

"Saint Francis of the Damned" was originally published in

ABOUT THE AUTHOR

A native Rhode Islander, **James Arthur Anderson** currently teaches English and literature at Johnson & Wales University's North Miami Campus at the rank of Professor. He earned his B.A. and M.A. from Rhode Island College, and his Ph.D. from the University of Rhode Island.

Dr. Anderson is the author of *The Altar*, a horror novel also set in Rhode Island, and the critical studies *The Illustrated Ray Bradbury*, and *Out of the Shadows*, all of which have been published by The Borgo Press. His poetry has appeared in literary journals published by Bryant University, Florida International University, and Texas Wesleyan University, to name just a few. His sonnet, "The Asian Market," won first place in the rhymed poetry category in the 76th annual Writer's Digest Writing Competition. He has also written articles for *Toastmaster* magazine, *Paso Fino Horse World*, *Alberta Bits*, and *Fangoria*.

When he is not writing or teaching, Jim can usually be found practicing his target shooting at the Hollywood Rifle and Pistol Club, or riding his spoiled horses in Davie, Florida with his wife Lynn.